# IS IT JUST?
by Minnie Smith

*Is It Just?*, a feminist domestic novel by Minnie Smith (ca. 1874–1934), is a harsh critique of the injustices perpetuated by male-dominated society and law. Published in 1911, it tells the tragic story of Mary Pierce, who, through the actions of her selfish and lazy husband, loses her land, her social standing, and ultimately her life.

In *Is It Just?*, the conventions of the domestic novel – episodic presentation, stock characters, contrived plots, and romantic conclusions – illustrate the superiority of female values and argue for expanded social, political, and legal rights for women. A critical introduction by Jenny Roth and Lori Chambers frames Smith's specific references to the laws and social geography of British Columbia, situating the novel in relation to its historical and literary importance. This unique work of domestic literature adds to our limited library of Canadian feminist writings of the first wave.

JENNY ROTH is an assistant professor in the Department of Women's Studies at Lakehead University.

LORI CHAMBERS is a professor in the Department of Women's Studies at Lakehead University.

# Is It Just?

## Minnie Smith

With a critical introduction by
Jenny Roth and Lori Chambers

UNIVERSITY OF TORONTO PRESS
Toronto Buffalo London

© University of Toronto Press Incorporated 2011
Toronto Buffalo London
www.utppublishing.com
Printed in Canada

ISBN 978-1-4426-1157-3

*Is It Just?* was first published in 1911 under the imprint of
William Briggs by the Methodist Book and Publishing House.

Printed on acid-free, 100% post-consumer recycled paper with
vegetable-based inks.

A cataloguing record for this publication is available from
Library and Archives Canada.

University of Toronto Press acknowledges the financial assistance to
its publishing program of the Canada Council for the Arts and the
Ontario Arts Council.

  Canada Council    Conseil des Arts      ONTARIO ARTS COUNCIL
for the Arts      du Canada                    CONSEIL DES ARTS DE L'ONTARIO

University of Toronto Press acknowledges the financial support of
the Government of Canada through the Canada Book Fund for its
publishing activities.

# Introduction

JENNY ROTH and LORI CHAMBERS

Minnie Smith's domestic novel about the legal perils of marriage, *Is It Just?*, was published in 1911 by the Methodist Book and Publishing House under the William Briggs imprint.[1] The book was dedicated to the National Council of Women and did not have extensive popular success, perhaps because it is much more strident in its critique of male-dominated society than the works of more famous women such as Nellie McClung. *Is It Just?* tells the tragic story of Mary Pierce (née Lee), whose selfish and lazy husband uses his legal right to their property to squander the family's monies. Mary Pierce loses her inheritance, the land that she had laboured to improve, and, temporarily, the respect of her community when her husband deserts her for another woman. Mary dies from a broken heart, despite the attempted interventions of her progressive daughter, her androgynous friend, and her repentant husband. Smith uses the conventions of the domestic novel – episodic presentation, stock characters, contrived plots, and romantic conclusions – to illustrate the superiority of female values and domestic virtues and to argue for expanded social, political, and legal rights for women. She sought, as others have argued with regard to Nellie McClung's fiction, to give voice to women 'kept silent by convention and socialization as well as fear, lack of education and plain bone-tiredness.'[2] Her work, although little known, is worthy of study. The novel adds to our as yet quite limited library of Canadian feminist writings of the first wave; it both uses and challenges the tropes of domestic literature; and it is an excellent case study of law in literature. Smith's dedication of the book and her specific references to the laws of British Columbia ensure that the novel has historical, as well as literary, importance.

## The Author

Little is known about Minnie Smith. She led a life of relative obscurity in Peachland, British Columbia, having earned a BA at McMaster College in Ontario in 1894.[3] She moved to the Okanagan with her brother and his family in the early twentieth century, taught school briefly, and was 'active in the Baptist Church.' Baptist archives note an obituary for 1934, although the obituary is not extant.[4] Minnie Smith was 'a member of the Woman's Christian Temperance Union and the Women's Institute.' Unmarried, she ran a successful fruit orchard and took an interest in local council and school board affairs. The novel was written 'in her spare time' and was her only published work of fiction.[5] She is described in local history accounts as 'indeed intelligent, and enjoyed a discussion, even to the point of argument, with the male sex especially.'[6] Her novel reflects this confrontational approach.

## The Domestic Novel and Feminist Protest

In the late nineteenth and early twentieth centuries, women agitators for rights and suffrage found the domestic drama to be an ideal vehicle through which to spread the tenets of maternal and equality feminism. From its emergence in the early nineteenth century with authors such as Jane Austen, the Brontës, Harriet Beecher Stowe, and Louisa May Alcott,[7] the domestic novel was dominated by women writers, and the popularity of the genre allowed women to make public arguments against their detractors, while safely writing appropriately 'feminine' subject matter about hearth, home, and women's strength in it.[8] For many years, domestic novels were dismissed by literary scholars as poor literature full of 'syrupy pathos, sentiment and optimism.'[9] With the rise of feminist literary criticism and critical feminist history, however, it is now recognized that these novels represented 'a monumental effort to reorganize culture from a woman's point of view'[10] and provided contemporary readers with 'alternative models for the conduct of their lives ... the exemplary novel therefore put into women's hands a powerful instrument of social change.'[11] Laurie Crumpacker notes that 'sentimental fiction could capitalize on a mass market, and domestic novels became early best-sellers. There was thus no more efficient way to disseminate reform, whether abolitionism, temperance, evangelicism, or women's rights, than through the popular fiction of the period.'[12]

The domestic novel was political because of, not in spite of, its focus on the home and family. The cultural construction of families as 'little Commonwealths,' the foundation of the state, body politic, and social order that appears in prescriptive texts from the Renaissance onward, meant that any writing which critiqued the state of the home could be read as a critique of patriarchal socio-political structures. While marriage is often the scene of the action in domestic novels, marriage must be understood as broadly as possible – as a political relationship between individuals that was affected by, and also affected, the State itself.[13] Elizabeth MacLeod Walls writes of New Woman literature in the early twentieth century: 'If the New Woman was a novelist who voiced progressive opinions, she also was a woman who did so indoors – inside the family and dominant culture. The New Woman rewrote the domestic novel instead of breaking the windows of Parliament to prove her point.'[14]

Most heroines of domestic fiction did not stray far from the ideal, maternal Angel in the House. Heroines were self-sacrificing, virtuous, moral women, driven by piousness and love for children and husbands. Mary Pierce, the long-suffering wife in *Is It Just?*, fits in this tradition. However, in Smith's novel the choices of this character are critiqued, thus challenging the ideals of maternal feminism. In most domestic novels, arguments for women's rights were mapped on to the pre-existing tropes of wife and mother. Smith goes beyond the loving mother imagery, with sympathetic and intelligent female characters who are unmarried: Mary Pierce's progressive daughter, Helen, and her radical, androgynous, single friend, the 'queer' Miss Todd. Minnie Smith's radicalism was exceptional. Her characters challenge not only patriarchal law, religion, and society but also many of the tropes and conventions of maternal feminism and domestic literature. This may explain both the failure of the novel as popular literature and its relative obscurity in the Canadian (feminist) canon today.

## Law and/in Literature

Domestic novels were important vehicles for legal critique. Novels, unlike other forms of protest, provided personal connection and emotionally charged examples of the problems that the law could create for women. As Nellie McClung diplomatically argued in 1915, 'The law is a reflection of public sentiment, and when people begin to realize that women are human and have human needs and ambitions and desires, the law will protect a woman's interest.'[15] The novel was a particularly powerful means of portraying women's 'human needs' to encourage support for legal change.

Law and literature scholars have long recognized that literature is a realm of the imaginary where complex legal subjects can exist to provide inroads that help us to understand how law, a seemingly extra-human institution, normalizes power structures and affects individuals. When authors challenged how the law bolstered traditional institutions of social control in their storylines, they offered readers a vision of a world that could be, one different from the world experienced day to day. As such, literary representations are not mimetic re-creations of the 'real' world; they are imagined worlds that can 'convert the given confines of the here and now into an open horizon of possibilities.'[16]

Smith and other early feminist writers revealed law to be a culturally bound, human institution that could be challenged and reworked. They also clearly connected the institution of law to other dominant discourses that bolstered it. In her introduction to *The Woman's Bible*, noted women's rights activist

Elizabeth Cady Stanton wrote that 'the canon law, the Scriptures, the creeds and codes and church discipline of the leading religions bear the impress of fallible man, and not of our ideal great first cause, "the Spirit of all Good," that set the universe of matter and mind in motion.'[17] When suffragists wrote within the socially acceptable realm of the sentimental domestic drama, they could question the status quo, accepted power relations, the culture that created the law, and the patriarchal ideology that oppressed women.

Suffragist authors supported the argument that legislation passed in patriarchal societies supports patriarchal institutions and power relations.[18] This creates a legal system that affects women and men in gender-specific ways, a 'sore thought' for Canadian suffragist Nellie McClung, who wrote in 1915: 'If any person doubts that the society of the present day has been made by men, and for men's advantage, let them look for a minute at the laws which govern society. Society allows a man all privilege, all license, all liberty, where women are concerned.'[19] Modern feminist jurisprudence, the feminist theory of law, asks: If law privileges one group, 'how could it be objective? If not objective, how could interpretation be impartial; and if not impartial, how could it be fair? ... how could it be fair to the marginalized and despised?'[20] But this is not a new question, as Minnie Smith asks through the character of Miss Todd with reference to the law: 'Is it just?' The novel is not unique in questioning the fairness of law. It is unique, however, in that it does so with regard to the specific state of marital property provisions in British Columbia.

### Marital Property Law and Reform in British Columbia

Minnie Smith and her contemporaries had much reason to complain with regard to the state of the law. The colonies of Vancouver Island and British Columbia inherited the legal institutions of England;[21] male control of property within marriage was nearly unfettered. As the eminent eighteenth-century jurist Sir William Blackstone put it, 'By marriage the husband and wife are one person in law: that is, the very being or legal existence of the woman is suspended during marriage, or at least incorporated and consolidated into that of the husband: under whose wing and cover she performs everything.'[22] As Blackstone also made clear, the unity of the married couple was premised on the subordination of the wife: she was 'so entirely under his power and control that she can do nothing of herself, but everything by his license and authority.'[23] A married woman could not sign a contract or enter into a business on her own account. Her personal property, even wages earned outside the home, belonged to her husband. While a married woman retained ownership of her real property – land – the husband had the right to manage such property for the duration of the marriage, and the wife could not even claim the rents or profits from the land (even when she needed such monies for necessaries). Even after the death of her husband a woman remained vulnerable, as he could will his own property to others, leaving her impoverished. In this context, wives were rendered financially dependent, obliging them to yield to masculine control.[24]

To prevent the dissipation of estates, the English legal system extended certain protections to wives and children. Wealthy families could place property in trust in the Court of Chancery, and by the late eighteenth century women were serving as trustees of their own equitable estates. Wives with property in trust could not sell their lands but could use the profits for survival. For those who could not afford to set aside a portion of family property in trust, the 'widow's third' – her common law right to dower – entitled the wife to the lifetime use of one-third of her husband's real estate. This not only protected some property for her use in the case of the husband's death but also gave her substantial control over the property during her husband's lifetime, as property could not be sold unless the wife had released her right to dower through formal proceedings. However, in the 1830s, the English Parliament abolished dower by statute, and this protection was therefore not available to wives in the colonies of Vancouver Island and British Columbia, where the law was received after the date of reform.[25] British Columbia also did not have a Court of Chancery.

Legislators in the colonies did not want to create dower rights or equitable trusts because they seriously inhibited the free and quick transfer of land ownership, a potential impediment to development in a frontier community.[26]

It was in this context that the first legislative reform of married women's property rights came in 1862 on Vancouver Island. The Deserted Wives' bill created a mechanism by which a deserted wife could apply to the courts for an order of protection. If granted, the order gave her the right to contract, sue, and be sued, and to hold her property against the claim of her husband, or his creditors.[27] In his excellent analysis of married women's property law reform in British Columbia, Chris Clarkson asserts that reform was prompted by concern for growing numbers of abused and deserted wives who might otherwise become a strain on the coffers of the colony.[28] The measure was modelled upon legislation that had already passed and been successfully implemented in Upper Canada/Ontario. It was carefully worded to maintain masculine prerogative in all but the most 'exceptional' of circumstances; property rights were dependent upon evidence that a husband had failed in his duty to provide for his family and could be obtained only through formal application.

Next, the government (now of British Columbia) passed a 'virtual duplicate of Ontario's 1872 Married Women's Property Act (MWPA).'[29] Under this act, married women were permitted to hold separately any real estate they possessed at the time of marriage, and to acquire or receive additional real property in their own names. They could acquire such property through gift or inheritance, or through wages from labour performed outside the home. Married women's separate property was to be held free from their husbands' control and debts.[30] Even this measure, however, provided limited freedom for wives. A wife might protect her property, including property conveyed to her as a gift from her husband, from her husband's creditors, but she did not have the right to alienate, sell, or encumber her land. This act, while denying women the right to alienate real estate, did improve the ability of a deserted or neglected wife to survive independently. She could control her wages and acquisitions after separation without the need for an order of protection. For intact families, however, the power of the husband was not seriously diminished by this measure. He continued to hold the right to his dependants' unpaid labour and controlled any income or property acquired through the collective efforts of family members.[31] Married women's unwaged contributions to the family were not recognized, and women gained no rights in family property. Moreover, any separate assets that a wife mingled with the goods of her husband in order to survive, or which she allowed him to take in his name, thereafter were considered to belong to him. Yet 'legislators were aware of the limits of married women's property rights and made a definite choice to extend them no further.'[32] Although dower bills were introduced in the legislature in both 1872 and 1873, these bills did not pass.[33] In 1887 a final Married Women's Property Act was passed, but it clarified and expanded the rights of creditors more than those of wives.[34]

It is not surprising in this context (and given the history of feminist organization in other jurisdictions) that property law was the first object of reform-minded, organized women in British Columbia. In 1910, the Vancouver University Women's Club hosted a talk by a lawyer who discussed the subject of women and the law; shortly thereafter, Helen Gregory MacGill became chair of the newly constituted Committee for Better Laws for Women and Children.[35] In Evlyn Farris's words, 'The members were very shocked to learn that in B.C. ... a man could leave his wife penniless.'[36] Their outrage prompted what Chris Clarkson describes as 'a sustained drive for legal reform,' and their failures 'contributed to mounting calls for women's suffrage.'[37] When the conservative provincial government fell in September 1916, women's suffrage and prohibition referendums passed, ushering in a new era of reform and the passage of mothers' pension legislation and deserted wives' and illegitimate children's maintenance laws,[38] but none of these addressed the issue faced by Mary Pierce – lack of control over marital property. Without dower rights or joint property, women remained vulnerable. It was this vulnerability that Minnie Smith abhorred and which she challenged in *Is It Just?*

The problem of exclusive male control over family property is the central theme of *Is It Just?* This theme is first introduced through Miss Todd, who has custody over her orphaned nieces and nephews because her sister died in poverty after her drunken husband gambled away their future. Miss Todd asks, 'Is it right, is it just, that our Western married women should work their fingers to the bone in their efforts to help their husbands in building homes only to find that they have no legal right to those same homes, to find that their husbands may, if they feel like it, mortgage everything, or even will all away from them without any redress?'[39] The problems soon to be faced by the Pierce family are foreshadowed when Miss Todd suggests to Mary Pierce that the family property should be in her name, 'for your children's sake, if not for your own, that you should see that you have some legal claim to this property.'[40] Mrs Pierce, however, responds indignantly: 'But my husband is neither a gambler nor a drunkard. Surely I can trust him to do the best he can for us all.'[41] Despite this automatic response, an 'unbidden thought told her, "Does not your past experience tell you that his best is very unsatisfactory? Your money bought this place, therefore you should have it in your own name."'[42] Mr Pierce, unlike stock male characters in most domestic protest novels, has more mundane flaws than drinking and gambling, but this does not save his family from destitution.

Mrs Pierce's worst fears are later realized when her husband is seduced by Mrs Yates, the young American widow with 'snaky eyes,'[43] mortgages the family property without telling his wife, and leaves her to attend to Mrs Yates in Chicago. If a man can be this easily tempted, Smith suggests, what right can he have to so much legal power? But Mrs Pierce, 'being one of the few women who know when it is wise to be silent, said no more.'[44] Smith is clearly sarcastic in this description; this represents the very silence that keeps women victimized and powerless within the family and in society at large. Mary, while wary, does not question her husband's decision: 'If you have fully made up your mind to go, I shall try my best to become reconciled to the idea. My home is where you and the children are, and I hope to find happiness in seeking to make that home a pleasant place, no matter where it may be.'[45] By being a 'good wife,' by keeping her silence, Mrs Pierce behaves in a manner that is antithetical to her own best interests and those of her children. In fact, she serves almost as a parody of the traditional ideal of wifely devotion and the stock mother character in domestic fiction. Walter Ong has observed that intertextuality is crucial to literature;[46] and suffragists' work spoke to and through each publication. Nellie McClung would later argue in 'Hardy Perennials' that women like Mrs Pierce are 'silly ladies': 'The shrinking violets will not be torn from their shady fence-corner; the "home bodies" will be able to still sit in rapt contemplation of their own fireside.'[47] Such stock characters, 'the self-sacrificial wife and mother,' as modern observers have commented, endured suffering that illustrates 'the emotional costs for women of their complicity in the construction and perpetuation of the domestic ideology.'[48]

Mary Pierce's situation goes from bad to worse after her husband departs, and when he is sent letters with unsubstantiated rumours of his wife's infidelity, he decides to divorce her. The double standard of sexual morality is clearly critiqued here: 'A man may allow his affections to stray to some unlawful object, but that does not tend to make him any more tolerant of infidelity on the part of his wife, whose duty is to love and cherish till death, whereas in his own opinion *his* duty is to love and cherish until he sees a fairer face.'[49] Through divorce, his wife loses her right even to remain on the farm, which her own money had purchased.[50] Smith argues that society colludes with law to disempower women: Mary Pierce is 'the unfortunate victim of slander, man's perfidy, woman's unscrupulousness, and British Columbia Law.'[51] She is saved from starvation only when an old friend (the one with whom she had been accused of infidelity) purchases the farm (and also offers to marry her). These experiences lead not only Miss Todd but also Helen, the eldest Pierce child, to assert that improved rights for women are necessary.

Miss Todd makes an impassioned argument for the right of women to the franchise. In answer to the fear that women will desert their homes if they vote, she argues that where women have the vote in municipal affairs, 'their homes are as well looked after as any home here where we have no municipality. At any rate, it is a violation of the fundamental principle of responsible government, "No taxation without representation," to deprive women who pay taxes of the right to say how those taxes should be spent; and an insult to their intelligence to class them with "criminals and idiots."'[52] Whether or not all women would vote is irrelevant: 'There are some men who seldom, if ever, vote. Should that fact rob all men of the franchise?'[53] And, on a more traditional note, a woman who thought deeply about political events and issues would be 'better qualified to instruct her children in the duties of citizenship.'[54] Miss Todd argues that women of good character would not be corrupted by participation in the political process; in fact, 'I think that politics would be purified by the introduction of women.'[55] Despite the veneration of women's domestic virtues and roles, women are silenced in the political process and are exceptionally vulnerable. These evils, according to Miss Todd, will not 'be removed until we women get our rights.'[56] These arguments, of course, are familiar to modern feminist readers, as they are the same assertions made by Nellie McClung in her famous treatise *In Times Like These*.

### Religion as Source of Law and Subject of Critique

Laws that erased married women and their rights took their authority from Christian teachings, and Minnie Smith, unlike most authors of domestic fiction, pointed directly to this problem. In the creation story in Genesis, marriage is established as the unification of husband and wife: 'man leaves his father and mother and is united with his wife and they become one.'[57] This one was clearly the husband. St Paul enjoined wives to 'submit yourselves to your husbands as to the Lord. For the husband has authority over his wife just as Christ has authority over the Church.'[58]

While a wife was to look to her husband as the Church to Christ, her legal erasure was built upon the earlier precedent established in the creation story. Because woman (Eve) did not adhere to the first 'law' that enjoined her not to eat the forbidden fruit, she proved that women, as a group, are incapable of following mandates and managing legal affairs. The author of *The Lawes Resolutions of Womens Rights* (1632), a compendium on women's rights under the common law, makes this clear in the third section, 'The Punishment of Adams Sinne': after 'eating the forbidden fruit: for which *Adam, Eve*, the serpent first, and lastly, the earth it selfe is cursed,' woman's *'desires shall bee subject to* [her] *husband, and he shall rule over'* her.[59] This is, he explains, 'the reason ... that Women have no voyce in Parliament. They make no Lawes, they consent to none, they abrogate none. All of them are understood either married or to bee married and their desires are subject to their husband. I know no remedy though some women can shift it well enough.'[60]

In this context, it is particularly important to note how often Smith challenges the creation story. The successful and independent Miss Todd lives on Canyon Ranch, one of 'several prosperous ranches' in the valley, which is directly referred to by Mr Pierce as 'quite a "Garden of Eden."'[61] His observation leads into the first of the verbal tussles that the two have during the Pierces' visit to Miss Todd's home; when Mr Pierce remarks that he sees no Eve on the ranch, Miss Todd asks, 'Where is the Adam?,' and Pierce answers, 'He is hiding somewhere.'[62] Miss Todd, spinster, successful rancher, and adoptive mother to her late sister's children, is no Eve; however, her 'Garden of Eden' suggests that life without men is prelapsarian. In fact, the only person to mention Eve throughout the novel is Guy Pierce; the women compare themselves to Adam,[63] perhaps making the connection between God's curse that condemned Adam to toil in pain and to work the earth to produce food by the sweat of his brow with their own hard work on their properties. Guy Pierce is lazy and disinterested, so his wife does the lion's share of the work, and the single Miss Todd has to be 'man and woman both on a fruit-ranch.'[64] In a twist that marks men as culpable for the Fall, by implication putting women on an equal footing with regard to legal autonomy and privilege, Guy Pierce is alternately represented as the serpent and Eve.

Suffragists were certainly aware of the negative effects that legal precedent and religious teachings had on women's position in society. *The Woman's Bible*, published in 1898, was a direct challenge to patriarchal readings of biblical passages and argued for a feminist rereading that would give women more rights. Elizabeth Cady Stanton wrote in her introduction: 'The canon and civil law; church and state; priests and legislators; all political parties and religious denominations have alike taught that woman was made after man, of man, and for man, an inferior being, subject to man. Creeds, codes, Scriptures and statutes, are all based on this idea.'[65] Suffragists 'rejected the Pauline doctrine of feminine inferiority' and included religious critique in their works.[66] This critique was particularly important; religious doctrine supported common law jurisprudence by arguing that as Christ is head of the Church, so the husband is head of his family. The conundrum is clear: husbands have the right to legal power because it is presumed they will perform their role, and perform it well, but the 'one person' paradigm only works when the husband is like Christ to the Church – when he cares for, protects, and nurtures his flock. St Paul asserted that a husband should 'love his wife as he loves himself. No one ever hates his own body. Instead he feeds and takes care of it.'[67] Smith's story makes plain to her readers that not all men fulfil their husbandly duties, and that for the wives of those men, there should be security. Unlike other suffragist representations of 'bad men' that were based on temperance arguments against drunkards and gamblers, Smith's Mr Pierce suggests a more radical reading: men did not need alcohol to make them bad or irresponsible, and too many men, often for mundane reasons, did not love their wives as they loved themselves.

Examples of Mr Pierce's ineptitude fill Smith's book, and they are often closely aligned with a critique of the religious teachings that lead to women's disempowerment in law. When the pious Mrs Pierce discovers that her husband has mortgaged the farm without telling her, 'for a few bitter moments it seemed to her that her love as well as her faith had received a blow from which it would never recover ... That he, whom she had so loved and trusted, could have mortgaged the place that had been bought with her own money, without saying a word to her, was indeed a bitter blow to her faith in him.'[68] Christian dogma inextricably intertwined faith in one's husband with faith in one's God (as the Church to Christ, wives were expected to place faith for their safe delivery in their husbands' hands). Miss Todd is exasperated by Mrs Pierce's blind faith in Mr Pierce: 'What simpletons some women are! If a man is good-looking and has a smooth tongue, no matter how black his heart may be, he will have half a dozen girls falling in love with him at a time.'[69] Miss Todd's description of the man as the 'smooth-tongued' malefactor who tempts young women to their fall inverts traditional assumptions about women's role in the Garden of Eden, the precedent that was used to justify women's subjection to men. Miss Todd rejects the doctrines that kept women legally bound to their husbands and rewrites them to make men culpable. Mary Pierce, not her husband, is likened to the sacrificing Christ at the end of the novel. Mr Pierce returns to the Okanagan to find his wife dying of heartache, and is told by the attending doctor: 'You might better have stabbed that loving wife of yours to the heart with a sword than have done such a dastardly trick as you did.'[70] Instead of the sacrificing father, it is the mother who suggests Christ on the cross, stabbed by attending soldiers.

Guy Pierce is not a good shepherd, nor does he tend his orchard carefully; a metaphorical connection between animal and plant husbandry and patriarchal husbandry runs throughout the novel. When the family begins to prepare the fruit trees on their newly purchased Okanagan farm, Pierce has difficulties first accessing water, and then ensuring that the water sent to his property is effective because he grows bored with waiting and returns home: 'Had Mr. Pierce been at his post all would have been well, but as he had deserted it in disgust, his ditches were now broken out and the freed water was wandering at its own sweet will, doing more harm than good.'[71] The disconnection between Pierce and the good husband is driven home in an argument between Mr Pierce and the successful Miss Todd when Pierce declares that he does not believe in the need for a Saviour.[72] Miss Todd argues for faith and caretaking – 'But do you not think your children are happier to know that you care what becomes of them than if they were to feel that you were perfectly indifferent to their welfare?' – to which Pierce responds, 'I don't think that has anything to do with the question at issue. But you are just like the rest of women, Miss Todd, always running off to a side-track. I never saw a woman that could really argue yet.'[73] From the perspective of feminist jurisprudence, Miss Todd's point is crucial: because the doctrine of a benevolent, caretaking Christ taught women it was God's will that they trust their husbands, Pierce's rejection of the need for a Saviour ominously foreshadows how he will mistreat his own family. He dismisses the woman's perspective as unimportant, unreasonable, and illogical, but Miss Todd makes the connection between failed husbandries when she later asks Mr Pierce, 'with a sly smile,' 'I wonder what kind of peaches I should have if I allowed the trees to manage themselves.'[74] Moreover, the exchange clearly reveals that women are capable, rational beings whose arguments are worthy of attention. The failed husbandries of men require a new womanhood, as Minnie Smith makes clear.

### 'The New Woman': Helen Pierce and Miss Todd

The Pierce family survives because of the selfless devotion, motherly love, and physical labour of women. These same women, however, are denied voice and power in both the family and society, and the legal power of the patriarch/father is largely unfettered. Helen Pierce, a model New Woman who transgresses gender boundaries and dreams of more equal status with men, expresses her discontent and resentment clearly. Her father too often makes decisions that endanger the whole family: 'I wish I were a man; then perhaps people would pay more attention to what I say.'[75] Helen Pierce watches her father squander her mother's inheritance in unsuccessful business ventures and then mortgage and sell the farm purchased with his wife's money without her knowledge. Helen's distrust of her father (and all things patriarchal) is proven correct when he deserts the family. Her nascent feminism is also encouraged by her growing friendship with Miss Todd, a neighbour who is very reminiscent of Minnie Smith herself, and who may be a partially autobiographical character.

Strong, independent, and single, Miss Todd runs a successful fruit orchard and is raising her sister's orphaned children. Very tall and conventionally unattractive, Miss Todd is androgynous: she has 'a decidedly conspicuous moustache on the upper lip. The square lower jaw showed firmness, and the bright, piercing eyes showed keen observation. Although most persons would have called her ugly, when Helen looked in her face as she greeted her, she was attracted rather than repelled.'[76] Miss Todd, industrious and 'nimble,' is not 'ladylike,' but this is not represented as a fault: 'I don't complain of my looks; I am as my Creator made me, and since He is satisfied, I am.'[77] Moreover, she personifies domestic, feminine virtues while also succeeding in the business world of men. She introduces herself to Helen as 'Miss Todd, not Mrs., thank heaven!'[78] Miss Todd's ranch is described as a Garden of Eden; her home is spotlessly clean and well appointed; and her children are well groomed, well behaved, and well educated.[79] Miss Todd represents the feminine ideal, for Minnie Smith, of self-sufficiency, independence, domesticity, and motherly love, an ideal that is achieved outside the traditional women's sphere of marriage. Although at the conclusion of the story Helen opts to marry, the portrayal of Miss Todd throughout the book suggests that this conclusion is used because it is the expected outcome of domestic fiction. Miss Todd is the only female character in the novel who achieves financial stability and personal happiness. For Smith, transformation of marriage (endorsed by many early twentieth-century women, including Nellie McClung) is insufficient, and perhaps impossible. Idyllic conditions can be achieved only when men are excluded altogether from the domestic realm; Miss Todd's ranch can survive as a Garden of Eden only because she admits no Adam.

Smith's character is linked to a small but notable tradition of independent and happy spinsters in the domestic novel: 'Grandmothers, who are beyond the dangers of pregnancy, and spinsters have a happier lot and a more powerful social role than wives and young mothers ... Spinster aunts and grandmothers in domestic novels are other models for and nurturers of the next generation, and it is the young people who demonstrate what the new generation of men and women might be ... talented people, regardless of their sex, and that they will also be able to marry and raise children without being destroyed in the process.'[80] Nellie McClung also argued for the spinster: 'That the term "old maid" has lost its odium is due to the fact that unmarried women have made a place for themselves in the world of business. They have become real people apart from their sex. The "old maid" of the past was a sad, anemic creature, without any means of support except the bounty of some relative ... The world is beginning to see that a woman may achieve success in other departments of life as well as marriage.'[81] Smith uses the spinster trope and Helen's admiration for Miss Todd to suggest a more egalitarian role for women and a more optimistic future for society. Helen's relationships with the 'New Men' of the novel also suggest a revisioning of masculinity and marriage.

### New Masculinities: Mr Hastings and Dick Hardy

Women did not work alone in their quest for equality, and male progressives were the 'new man' to the early twentieth-century's 'new woman.' Shifting masculinities were thus also a recurring theme in some New Woman literature.[82] Smith reveals the connections between a legal system that privileges men and men's sense of entitlement to social dominance through the character of Guy Pierce and critiques that sense of entitlement with the more sensitive and equality-minded characters of Mr Hastings and his nephew, Dick Hardy. The law as it was constituted endorsed the power of irresponsible men like Guy Pierce and treated women as mere property. However, New Woman writers recorded a new masculinity that promised a hopeful future. New men, potential and future husbands of new women, saw women as equals and partners. Both Philip Hastings and Dick Hardy represent this more hopeful version of masculinity. Hastings is financially successful, 'wealthy,' and 'respected,' and, importantly, 'children and dogs loved him.'[83]

The two marriages in the novel, the first between Mary Lee and Guy Pierce, and the second, the promised nuptials between

Helen Pierce and Dick Hardy, follow the domestic novel's trope of second generations holding more optimistic futures. Before she married Mr Pierce, Mary Lee had another potential suitor, Philip Hastings. He was clearly the 'good man' to her 'good woman.' She won him over with her tender nursing after he was attacked by her horse.[84] He is a successful rancher and one of 'Nature's gentlemen' with 'clear grey eyes' and a 'strong face.'[85] By contrast, the young Mr Pierce 'belonged to that class rather contemptuously regarded by their neighbors as "remittance men." Depending upon money sent from relatives in the Old Country, Pierce saw no reason why he should hurt himself working.'[86] After Hastings recovered from his wounds, he became a regular visitor at the Lee farm, until he was surprised one night 'by a visit from Mr. Pierce,' who, after a tense exchange between the two men, announced that he and Mary Lee were engaged.[87] It is quickly apparent that Mary Lee has made the wrong choice: Pierce gloats vainly over his looks, mocks Philip Hastings' scar from the horse attack, and admits to Hastings that it is Mary's inheritance that he loves, not her.[88]

The difference between the two men continues to play out in the latter part of the novel when Mr Hastings moves his operation from Manitoba to the Okanagan to protect Mary after her mistreatment at the hands of Guy Pierce. Before Pierce returns to the Okanagan, Mr Hastings offers to marry Mrs Pierce and to provide for her family, but Mary Pierce not only asserts (in the tradition of the good and loyal wife that is presented with irony throughout the novel) that she still loves her husband but also denigrates herself: 'I have no husband. I am that most miserable and despised being, a divorced woman.' Hastings responds, 'You are a free woman,'[89] redefining the trope that made women, married women in particular, property. When Mrs Pierce rejects Mr Hastings' marriage proposal, Smith again critiques the woman who chooses culturally defined morality over common sense. Mary Pierce could easily provide for her children were she to accept Mr Hastings' offer.

Although Mary (Lee) Pierce chooses the wrong man throughout her life, her daughter Helen does not, and it is this vision of hope offered by the second generation that suffragists wanted to disseminate as an alternative way of life. Like his Uncle

Philip, Dick Hardy is represented as a hard-working, honest man; he 'was a tall, broad-shouldered young man of twenty-five, whose broad forehead and clear [and later 'honest'] grey eyes denoted intelligence, and tightly pressed lips and square-ly-built jaw, determination.'[90] He has a 'firm but gentle grasp' and does not hesitate to offer Helen help around the farm.[91] Helen at first rejects his proposal, but Miss Todd finally con-vinces her to marry Hardy, and it is clear that this second mar-riage will be successful. Whereas Guy Pierce implicitly rejected the divine ordinances (and responsibilities) connected with matrimony, Helen's marriage is based on 'that love which God has planted in [her] heart.'[92]

Despite the strong feminist themes of the novel, its conclu-sion is conventional to the point of seeming contrived. Guy Pierce, who has realized too late his error in deserting Mary, returns only in time to clear her name of scandal by remarry-ing her after a divorce from his Chicago wife, and to attend her on her deathbed. Mary welcomes him back with open arms despite warning signs that he has not changed. Although filled with anxious remorse, he blames Mrs Yates' 'false face that lured [him] to destruction,' not his own perfidy for the destruc-tion of their marriage.[93] Helen, the new woman, is not fooled by his repentance, however: 'If it had not been for the fear of wounding her mother's feelings, Helen would have expressed her indignation at her father's daring to return to the home whose happiness he had wrecked.'[94] Guy Pierce's return does, however, remove disgrace from the family name so that Helen can agree to marry the man she loves, Dick Hardy. The novel closes on a note of traditional sentimentality and optimism, which, although incongruous with the preceding story, builds on the new woman and new man ideals and follows the do-mestic drama trope of placing hope and optimism with second generations.

## Conclusion

Minnie Smith was a crusader for women's rights and used lit-erature as a form of propaganda. Although *Is It Just?* is not great literature, it is nonetheless important literature. It is within its political context that the work must be judged. As Hélène Cixous points out in one of her many works on subject formation: 'The repressive machine has always had the same accomplices: homogenizing, reductive, unifying reason has always been an ally of the Master, of the one Subject, stable and socializable; and it is here, at the base of it all, that literature has already been striking blows, where the theses and concepts of Order imposed themselves, by denouncing them on the level of the signified.'[95]

Universal, monolithic legal discourse obscures 'the fact that its history, decisions, and stories could have developed in a different manner, taking in other experiences, other views, other voices';[96] literature can give voice to those often silenced by law and can reveal law's contradictions and arbitrariness. Smith uses the domestic novel to give voice to suffrage arguments that called for women's rights and empowerment of women within marriage, in particular 'just' arrangements regarding family property. Because literary texts represent worlds where anything is possible,[97] they are a perfect 'medium for jurisprudential debate.'[98] Any literary text is always political because it either reinforces social power structures or challenges them. Because literature can suggest different social orders, characters are often more multidimensional than subjects constructed by law. Miss Todd, the unconventional 'old maid' in Smith's novel, challenges the legal and social construction of women as unknowledgeable, irresponsible, and politically naïve. Miss Todd's successful independence illustrates how literature is 'more likely than law to challenge received ideologies, values, and prejudices'[99] through its characters' words and actions. The legal subject in literature can be much more complex than its empirical counterpart. The values approved of in law 'may well differ very considerably from day-to-day practices,'[100] which are more easily represented in literature. Although extant laws implicitly constructed women as inept, Miss Todd illustrates that women clearly are not. How such fictitious legal subjects interact with legislated hierarchies is what makes literature worthwhile in a cultural criticism of the law. This is also why *Is It Just?*, an obscure but radical early twentieth-century example of the domestic novel as feminist protest, is worthy of historical, as well as literary, interest.

NOTES

1 It is interesting that a religious publishing house would involve itself in the publication of such material. This is suggestive of the connections between temperance, legal reform, the social gospel, and the movement for women's rights.

2 Misao Dean, 'Voicing the Voiceless: Language and Genre in Nellie McClung's Fiction and Her Autobiography,' *Atlantis* 15(1) (Autumn 1989), 65.

3 Canadian Baptist Archives, personal communication, 25 February 2010.

4 Ibid.

5 Peachland Historical Association, *Peachland Memories: A History of the Peachland and Trepanier Districts in the Beautiful Okanagan Valley* (Kelowna, BC: Ehmann Printing, 1980), 577–8.

6 Ibid., 578.

7 Nancy Armstrong, 'The Rise of Feminine Authority in the Novel,' *Novel: A Forum on Fiction* 15(2) (Winter 1982), 127–45; Laurie Crumpacker, 'Four Novels of Harriet Beecher Stowe: A Study in Nineteenth-Century Androgyny,' in *American Novelists Revisited: Essays in Feminist Criticism*, ed. F. Fleischmann (Boston: Hall, 1982); Solveig C. Robinson, '"Amazed at Our Success": The Langham Place Editors and the Emergence of a Feminist Critical Tradition,' *Victorian Periodicals Review* 29(2) (Summer 1996), 159–72.

8 Mary Vipond, 'Best Sellers in English Canada, 1899–1918: An Overview,' *Journal of Canadian Fiction* 24 (1979), 73–105.

9 James D. Hart, *The Popular Book: A History of America's Literary Taste* (New York: Oxford University Press, 1950), 203.

10 Jane Tompkins, *Sensational Designs: The Cultural Work of American Fiction, 1790–1860* (New York: Oxford University Press, 1985), 123.

11 Eve Tavor Bannet, *The Domestic Revolution: Enlightenment Feminisms and the Novel* (Baltimore: Johns Hopkins University Press, 2000), 10.

12 Crumpacker, 'Four Novels of Harriet Beecher Stowe,' 79.

13  See, for example, Danielle Clarke, '"This domestic kingdome or monarchy": Cary's *The Tragedy of Mariam* and the Resistance to Patriarchal Government,' *Medieval and Renaissance Drama in England* 10 (1998), 179–200; Jennifer Phegley, *Educating the Proper Woman Reader: Victorian Family Literary Magazines and the Cultural Health of the Nation* (Columbus: Ohio State University Press, 2004).

14  Elizabeth MacLeod Walls, '"A Little Afraid of the Women of Today": The Victorian New Woman and the Rhetoric of British Modernism,' *Rhetoric Review* 21(3) (2002), 238.

15  Nellie McClung, 'The Sore Thought,' *In Times Like These* (Toronto: University of Toronto Press, [1915] 1972), 92.

16  Richard Kearney, *Poetics of Imagining: Modern to Post-Modern,* new ed. (Edinburgh: Edinburgh University Press, 1998), 2. See also Wolfgang Iser, 'Representation: A Performative Act,' in *The Aims of Representation: Subject/Text/History,* ed. Murray Krieger (Stanford: Stanford University Press, 1987).

17  Elizabeth Cady Stanton, Introduction, *The Woman's Bible,* Great Minds Series (Amherst, NY: Prometheus Books, [1898] 1999), 13.

18  Frances Olsen, 'The Sex of Law,' in *The Politics of Law: A Progressive Critique,* 3rd ed., ed. David Kairys (New York: Basic Books, 1998), 701.

19  McClung, 'The Sore Thought,' 84.

20  Guyora Binder, 'The Law-as-Literature Trope,' in *Law and Literature,* ed. Michael Freeman and Andrew D.E. Lewis, Current Legal Issues 1999, vol. 2 (Oxford: Oxford University Press, 1999), 71.

21  Each North American British colony inherited English law as it existed at the date of the creation of the colony. Vancouver Island became a colony in 1851; British Columbia in 1858; and the colonies were merged in 1866. From that time, British law as it existed in 1858 applied to the entire colony, although such laws could be altered by local statute. The laws of the province did not change when British Columbia entered Confederation in 1871. See Chris Clarkson, *Domestic Reforms: Political Visions and Family Regulation in British Columbia, 1862–1940* (Vancouver: UBC Press, 2007), and Margaret McCallum, 'Prairie Women and the Struggle for Dower Law, 1905–1920,' *Prairie Forum* 18(1) (1993).

22  Sir William Blackstone, *Commentaries on the Laws of England, in Four Books,* vol. 2, ed. George Tucker, (1803), reprinted New York,

1969, 242. Although the *Commentaries* presented a simplified version of the law, Norma Basch has argued forcefully that this simplified form became the educational staple of a generation of American lawyers and informed basic interpretations of the common law; Norma Basch, *In the Eyes of the Law: Women, Marriage and Property in Nineteenth Century New York* (Ithaca: Cornell University Press, 1982), ch. 2.

23  Blackstone, *Commentaries*, 433.

24  For a full description of the status of the married woman, see Clarkson, *Domestic Reforms*; Constance Backhouse, 'Married Women's Property Law in Nineteenth-Century Canada,' *Law and History Review* 6(2) (Fall 1988); and Lori Chambers, *Married Women and Property Law in Victorian Ontario* (Toronto: University of Toronto Press and the Osgoode Society for Canadian Legal History, 1997).

25  Eileen Spring, *Law, Land and Inheritance: Aristocratic Inheritance in England, 1300–1800* (Chapel Hill: University of North Carolina Press, 1993); Catherine Cavanaugh, 'The Limitations of the Pioneering Partnership: The Alberta Campaign for Homestead Dower, 1909–25,' *Canadian Historical Review* 74(2) (1993); and McCallum, 'Prairie Women and the Struggle for Dower Law.'

26  Legislation passed in British Columbia was not unique to the province; married women's property law reform was widespread in England and the North American states and provinces throughout the second half of the nineteenth century.

27  Clarkson, *Domestic Reforms*, ch. 1. British Columbia, *The Laws of British Columbia, Consisting of the Acts, Ordinances & Proclamations of the Formerly Separate Colonies of Vancouver Island and British Columbia, and the United Colony of British Columbia,* by Authority Compiled and Published by the Commissioners Appointed under 'The Revised Statutes Act, 1871' (Victoria: Government Printer, 1871), 54–5.

28  Clarkson, *Domestic Reforms*, ch. 1.

29  Ibid., ch. 3.

30  Ibid., and Chambers, *Married Women and Property Law*, ch. 5.

31  Sara L. Zeigler, 'Wifely Duties: Marriage, Labor, and the Common Law in Nineteenth-Century America,' *Social Science History* 20(1) (Spring 1996), 67.

32  Clarkson, *Domestic Reforms*, ch. 4.
33  Arthur Bunster called on the legislature to enact a Dower Bill,
    which would have provided married women with secure legal
    rights in their husbands' realty. His 1872 bill was a short docu-
    ment, containing only two clauses: the first provided a wife with
    an inalienable dower right in one-third of the property her hus-
    band had held during her coverture; the second stipulated that
    the husband could not mortgage, dispose, or otherwise alienate
    his real property without the consent of his wife, and that every
    instrument of conveyance must specify whether the wife was
    releasing her dower claim. Ibid., ch. 4.
34  Ibid.
35  Ibid., ch. 5.
36  Tammy Adilman, 'Evlyn Farris and the University Women's
    Club,' in *In Her Own Right: Selected Essays on Women's History in
    B.C.*, ed. Barbara Latham and Cathy Kess (Victoria: Camosun
    College, 1980), 155.
37  Clarkson, *Domestic Reforms*, ch. 5.
38  Ibid., ch. 6.
39  Minnie Smith, *Is It Just?*, 51. All page references are to this
    volume.
40  Ibid., 53.
41  Ibid.
42  Ibid.
43  Ibid., 106.
44  Ibid., 78.
45  Ibid., 89.
46  Walter Ong, *Orality and Literacy: The Technologizing of the Word*
    (New York: Routledge, 1989).
47  McClung, 'Hardy Perennials,' *In Times Like These*, 56.
48  Lyn Pykett, *The 'Improper Feminine': The Women's Sensation Novel
    and the New Woman Writing* (London: Routledge, 1992), 150.
49  Smith, *Is It Just?*, 103–4.
50  Ibid., 105.
51  Ibid., 108.
52  Ibid., 66.
53  Ibid.
54  Ibid., 66–7.

55  Ibid., 69.
56  Ibid., 65.
57  Genesis 2:24.
58  Ephesians 5:22.
59  Anonymous, *The Lawes Resolutions of Womens Rights: or, The Lawes Provision for Woemen* (London, 1632), 6. Original text reads 'thy.'
60  Ibid.
61  Smith, *Is It Just?*, 56.
62  Ibid., 57.
63  Ibid., 56–7; 61.
64  Ibid., 48.
65  Stanton, Introduction, *The Woman's Bible*, 7.
66  Veronica Strong-Boag, 1972 Introduction to McClung, *In Times Like These*, viii.
67  Ephesians 5:28–9.
68  Smith, *Is It Just?*, 93.
69  Ibid., 114.
70  Ibid., 133.
71  Ibid., 35.
72  Ibid., 62.
73  Ibid., 63.
74  Ibid.
75  Ibid., 23.
76  Ibid., 47.
77  Ibid.
78  Ibid.
79  Ibid., 57.
80  Crumpacker, 'Four Novels of Harriet Beecher Stowe,' 99–100.
81  McClung, 'The Sore Thought,' 86.
82  Luisa Maria Flora, 'Identity, Gender and Fishing Flies: George Egerton's "A Cross Line,"' in *The Crossroads of Gender and Century Endings*, ed. Alcinda Pinheiro de Sousa et al. (Lisbon, Portugal: Colibri, 2000), 95–110.
83  Smith, *Is It Just?*, 19.
84  Ibid., 15–16.
85  Ibid., 14.
86  Ibid., 16.
87  Ibid., 17.

88  Ibid., 18.
89  Ibid., 110.
90  Ibid., 120, 121.
91  Ibid., 121.
92  Ibid., 131.
93  Ibid., 125.
94  Ibid., 127.
95  Hélène Cixous, *The Hélène Cixous Reader*, ed. Susan Sellers (London and New York: Routledge, 1994), 32.
96  Maria Aristodemou, *Law and Literature: Journeys from Her to Eternity* (Oxford: Oxford University Press, 2000), 26.
97  Jacques Derrida, *Acts of Literature*, ed. Derek Attridge (New York and London: Routledge, 1992), 36–8.
98  Ian Ward, *Law and Literature: Possibilities and Perspectives* (Cambridge: Cambridge University Press, 1995), 9.
99  Aristodemou, *Law and Literature*, 9.
100 Catherine Belsey, *Shakespeare and the Loss of Eden: The Construction of Family Values in Early Modern Culture* (London: Macmillan, 1999), 6.

# IS IT JUST?

By
### MINNIE SMITH

DEDICATED

TO

THE NATIONAL COUNCIL OF WOMEN

# CONTENTS

# CONTENTS

# IS IT JUST?

## CHAPTER I.

### *THE LAND AGENT'S VISIT.*

" MOTHER, when are we going to have supper?
The table has been set for ever so long and I'm
dreadfully hungry."

The speaker was a little ten-year-old boy whose
rosy cheeks and robust form showed him to be
the possessor of good health. His dark eyes—so dark
that they were often taken for black—and his pout-
ing lips spoke impatience as much as his ready
tongue.

· " Why, Harry, surely you don't want supper without your father! He may be here at any minute, and
you know, dear, he does not like to have his meals
alone, if it can be helped," was the answer given by
Mrs. Pierce to her quick-tempered boy, who had
tossed the book he had been reading upon the well-
worn lounge on which he was sitting.

" It's a quarter to seven, and I don't hear the bells
yet. There's somebody coming in now, perhaps it's
Dad. Pshaw! it's only Helen coming in from the
stable."

A girl of about fourteen, who, in spite of her heavy coat, shivered when she came into the warm room, which in the winter was both kitchen and dining-room, put the pail of milk upon the wooden bench that occupied the greater part of one side of the room, and came to the stove to warm her hands.

Let us look at her as she stands thus engaged. Only a Manitoba farmer's daughter and maid of all work as well; in spite of her rather irregular features and a nose that seems too large for her face, there is something very attractive in Helen's countenance. Her complexion is good—health and plenty of fresh air being the only cosmetics—and her lips and chin indicate firmness, while a slight dimple in each cheek shows a little love of mischief; but her eyes are her attraction. Dark grey and very large, protected by long eyelashes, there is something in their expression that at once wins a person's confidence.

Although she is still a child, she has had a wo-man's—nay, often a man's—work to do already in her short life. Somebody asks how this could be. On a Manitoba farm, or indeed on any Canadian farm, there is always plenty of work to do, and if there is no hired help and the husband and father has an aversion to hard work, then the burden must fall upon the wife and children.

"Mother," said Helen, taking off her tam and coat, "it is turning very cold; the wind is rising fast and I am afraid we are going to have another bliz-zard!"

"Oh, I hope not! We have had three already this winter and it is now nearly the end of March.

But I do wish your father would come home. His cold won't be improved by the night air."

" I don't think, mother, he is as sick as you. You ought to be in bed and not working like a slave," was Helen's response, spoken in rather a bitter tone.

" Please, mother, let us have supper, I'm getting sleepy. Daddy may not be home for another hour. Maybe he's had his supper at Souris. Then we'll have had our long wait for nothing," said May, the six-year-old pet of the family.

As May generally got her own way, Mrs. Pierce concluded to wait no longer for the missing head of the family; so, much to the contentment of hungry Harry, the mother and children sat down to the bountiful meal, with appetites sharpened by the long delay. But before they were half through, sleigh bells were heard rapidly approaching the house.

"There's Daddy at last! I know our bells. Run out with the lantern, Harry. Hurry, don't keep him waiting this cold night. You can finish your supper afterwards."

Harry, with a rather poor grace, obeyed his elder sister's command, slamming the door as he went out.

In a few minutes the stamping of feet was the signal of the arrival of Mr. Pierce. But he was not alone. To his wife's astonishment, mingled with dismay, a well-dressed stranger accompanied the head of the household.

" I hope he isn't going to stay the night, for I am sure I don't know where to put him," was the involuntary thought of the wife as the husband introduced the stranger to her as a Mr. Masson, from British Columbia.

" I do think you might have waited for me a little
longer. You know how I hate to sit down at the
table when there's nothing much to be seen but a
soiled tablecloth and dirty dishes. The little appe-
tite I had is all gone now, I am sure," was the vexed
greeting vouchsafed Mrs. Pierce after the introduction was over. The tired woman could hardly keep
the tears from coming into her eyes; it was certainly
very humiliating to be found fault with in the presence of a stranger. But she quietly instructed Helen
to remove the offending dishes, and to put some more
hot victuals on the table. In spite of Mr. Pierce's
grumbling remarks, he, as well as the stranger, did
ample justice to the meal.

While they are so engaged, let me describe the two
men. It would have been difficult in any ordinary
neighborhood to find a handsomer man than Mr.
Pierce. Tall, and with the chest and shoulders of an
athlete, a well-shaped head, covered with wavy hair
of golden-brown hue, a low but broad forehead, features of a classic regularity, and eyes whose color
perplexed the onlooker, but whose beauty nobody
could deny, he certainly possessed some claims to
good looks. Many a young lady often envied him
his remarkably clear skin. Indeed, many people
wondered how such an Apollo could have married so
plain and insignificant a person as his wife. But
there was an attractive something about the little
woman's face that the keenest observer failed to find
in that of her husband.

Now let us look at the stranger. Mr. Masson was
a rather short man, coming only to the shoulder of
his host, but what he lacked in height he made up in

breadth. He had a round jovial face and an expression that showed his satisfaction with himself and the world in general.

"Well, Mary, I have made up my mind to leave this inhospitable climate. My health will not allow me to spend another winter here; and I am sure you will be only too glad to go to a country where you won't have to smother yourself with wraps when you call upon your neighbors in the winter," said Mr. Pierce to his wife after the children had retired for the night.

"I don't mind the winters here much. We are quite comfortable, and I dread moving," was the quiet remark of the wife as she thought to herself, "I suppose this gentleman is a land agent, and has talked Guy into going to British Columbia. I do wish Guy could settle down long enough for us to feel that we have a home and that we are not gypsies. We are beginning to feel attached to this place and to have many of the comforts, if not the luxuries, of life around us, when the moving fever attacks him for the fifth time since our marriage."

"My dear Mrs. Pierce, do you not wish to live where you will enjoy all the comforts you have here without having to undergo the trials of the long and bitter winter? Just think! it is thirty degrees below zero now, and the wind blows as if it were getting ready for a blizzard. This very night I am sure my folks at home have the doors and windows open, enjoying the pleasant breezes of Lake Okanagan, one of the most beautiful sheets of water in the world. All last winter my little girls went half a mile to school barehanded and bareheaded. Wife and I

couldn't persuade them to wear coats, they wouldn't
be bothered with them. A year ago to-day we finished planting our potatoes, but there are no signs of
spring here yet," was Mr. Masson's rejoinder, rapidly
spoken, as if the speaker were afraid some person
might interrupt him before he would have time to
release the words that, like prisoners unexpectedly
set free, seemed hurrying over one another in their
anxiety for freedom.

"A most delightful climate, I assure you, my
dear! You surely would not wish to remain here
another winter when my health, perhaps my life, is
at stake," said the host when Mr. Masson stopped
to take breath.

"It is astonishing, the number of consumptives
who come to our Canadian Italy for relief from
their sufferings. Many of them have recovered, and
others are feeling so much better that life is becoming a pleasure to them. The air is so pure and bracing that asthma, hay fever, and rheumatism are not
known there except when persons who are afflicted
with these diseases come for their health to this
Canadian Mecca. Just think, my dear madam, how
pleasant it will be for you, your estimable husband,
and your lovely and intelligent children to enjoy
beautiful scenery, delightful companionship, unri-
valled facilities for communication with other places,
electric light, unsurpassed educational advantages,
and all the necessary modern conveniences."

"I doubt very much whether we could make a
living there as easily as we do here," was Mrs.
Pierce's reply to the agent's glowing eulogy.

" As easily! Why, my dear Mrs. Pierce, you can make a much better one with only half the trouble. You buy a ten-acre lot at $100 or $150 an acre, according to location, lay out, say eight acres in fruit trees, reserving the rest for building and garden; plant tomatoes, vegetables and small fruit between your rows and you will make $200 an acre every year until the trees bear. In the case of peach trees, they have been known to bear a crate per tree when only two years old. In five years after planting your orchard, you will be getting an income of $1,200 or $1,500 from your fruit trees alone. Your place will have increased in value 500 per cent., and you will have all the fruit you want and a good income with very little work."

" That's the part that suits me," said Mr. Pierce, with a half laugh, " hard work and I don't agree. Here I've been working like a slave on this cursed ranch for five years and I'm no better off to-day than I was when we came here. We won't have any trouble in selling. I saw a man to-day who will buy our ranch and pay cash for it, too."

" How much will he give?" asked his wife.

" Five thousand dollars for the place, including stock and implements."

" That's rather cheap, I think. The fruit trees must bear much better in British Columbia than they did on our Ontario farm to produce the income you speak of, Mr. Masson."

" So they do, so they do. A friend of mine has apple trees that brought him an average of $15 a tree. It is nothing uncommon for peach trees

to yield ten or twelve crates of first-class
fruit each. Irrigated land yields surer and
larger crops than non-irrigated. I see you're getting the B.C. fever as well as your husband. I advise you to take the offer made him, and come to the
Okanagan as soon as you can get away. Land is
rising so fast that you will do well to buy from me
while I am here. I am sure that I have some that
will just suit you. Land worth two months ago only
$10 an acre is selling at $100 or more. Nothing
like taking time by the forelock, you know."

Almost persuaded that it would be advantageous
to move to this much-praised country, Mrs. Pierce,
after seeing that the bedroom for the guest was comfortable, retired to rest. To rest, did I say? Yes,
if a night spent in dreaming about peach trees laden
with downy, luscious fruit; of apple trees bending
with the weight of rosy-cheeked apples; of water-
melons rolling down side hills, and burying her
alive; of wading through strawberries whose juice
stained her clothes, but whose flavor she did not enjoy,
as, no sooner did she attempt to pick a berry than it
seemed to be pulled back by some mysterious agency,
can be favorable to rest.

The three succeeding days kept Mr. Masson, by no
means an unwilling prisoner, in the small but cosy
Manitoba farm-house. A regular blizzard made it
unsafe for any person to venture out of sight of shelter. The men had to keep firm hold of a rope
fastened for that special purpose to the house and
barn, when they went to the stable to attend to the
cattle and horses. During his confinement, the agent

used his nimble tongue to such good purpose that
the Pierces became purchasers of a partly-improved
ten-acre lot at Ortgeard for the sum of $3,000.
" Dirt cheap " it was, according to Mr. Masson, and
a fortune lay ahead of them, if half of what he
prophesied should come true.

# CHAPTER II.

## PHILIP HASTINGS.

NOT ten miles from the Pierce farm lived a bachelor on an 800-acre ranch. His out-buildings, dwelling-house, stock, and the general appearance of the whole farm showed the thrift and intelligence of the owner, Philip Hastings. Although an Englishman, having lived in Manitoba for more than twenty years, he regarded Canada as his own country, by adoption, if not by birth. The bracing air and the wide, billowy prairie, studded with countless blossoms of varied hue, and the sunny sky, seemed to have made this man, whom nobody could call handsome, one of "Nature's gentlemen." No person could look into his clear grey eyes and at his strong face without saying to himself: "There's a man I can trust." In spite of his worldly prosperity, there was an expression on his face that told the careful observer that thorns as well as roses had strewed his pathway. He rarely smiled, but when he did, his whole face brightened, so that those who were fortunate enough to see him then forgot his long nose, his large mouth, and the scar that slightly disfigured his left cheek, and called him "quite good looking." To the few who knew how Mr. Hastings obtained this scar, it was a badge of honor.

14

Hastings was riding, when he heard the sound of galloping hoof-beats rapidly coming behind him. A girl's frightened cry told him that something was wrong. Hastily turning around, he saw that the flying steed was utterly beyond the control of its young rider. It was the work of a few moments to jump from his own horse and dash over to stop the runaway before it should dash its mistress against one of the large cottonwood trees for which it was now heading. Philip was just in time to save the girl; but the maddened animal, furious at being mastered by a stranger in its endeavor to get free, laid open the cheek of its conqueror. The young girl, instead of screaming, as most young ladies would have done, as soon as she saw the blood streaming from her deliverer's face, insisted on bathing it with water that she got from the brook that rippled near the spot where the accident occurred. Taking off the veil that fastened her hat, she deftly bound it over the dainty handkerchief she had used in bathing the wound. This improvised bandage would not have disgraced a trained nurse, although it certainly did not improve the patient's appearance.

Although so badly hurt, Mr. Hastings would not leave his new acquaintance until he saw her safely mounted on her horse, which now seemed under perfect control.

The acquaintance thus formed soon ripened into friendship on the part of the girl, and into a warmer feeling on the part of the young man. He could not forget the expression of kind sympathy in the sweet face of the girl, and the womanly and delicate touch of her hands while she ministered to his needs; she naturally felt a grateful interest in him who had risked his life to save her from almost certain death.

Mr. Hastings appreciated the kindness of Miss Lee in frequently sending a messenger to Poplar Grove—such was the name given to his place—to inquire how the wounded cheek was progressing, and also to ask if any help were needed. She even came herself one sunny afternoon to see him and quite won the graces of the rather " crusty " housekeeper by her skill as a cook in preparing a dainty dish for the sufferer.

Of course, after his recovery, he felt it his duty to return the gracious call of his fair visitor. He found her and her father such agreeable companions that his visits became so frequent that his housekeeper, Mrs. Hicks, used to say to herself, " I s'pose Mr. Hastings won't need me much longer. Well, I don't care; she'll make him a good wife, and if ever a man deserved one, Philip Hastings does. As for me, I can easy get another place, 'tho 'twill be hard for me to find people so ready to put up with my short temper as my young master. Bless his sunny face, anyway, I say."

About two miles from Poplar Grove was the preemption of Mr. Guy Pierce, another Englishman, but one who belonged to that class rather contemptuously regarded by their neighbors as " remittance men." Depending upon money sent from relatives in the Old Country, Pierce saw no reason why he should hurt himself working; so his place saw less of him than did the neighboring town or the Lees, whose home he frequently visited.

One evening in the fall Philip was surprised by a visit from Mr. Pierce. Surprised, as, although the two were fellow-countrymen, they were so dissimilar in their tastes and habits that they were not disposed to be particular friends. After the customary greetings, Mr. Pierce soon disclosed his errand by this abrupt remark, " I should like to know, Mr. Hastings, your reasons for your frequent visits to the Lees."

" I did not know I was accountable to you for my actions, nor do I see why you have any right to ask my reasons for visiting the Lees, or any other place as often as I see fit," was the indignant answer to the insolent remark.

" I have every right to ask you. When I tell you that Miss Lee and I are engaged to be married, your sense of honor, which is said to be so keen, will show you the impropriety of such frequent visits on your part. Ah! I see I have made you wince," said Pierce, with a sneer.

Keenly as he realized his bitter disappointment, Philip was too much the master of his emotions to allow his rival to see that he was undergoing the bitterest trial of his life. A look of pain in his clear grey eyes, and his tightly-pressed lips, alone showed Pierce that the arrow was doing its work.

After a minute's silence, Philip calmly answered his tormentor, " I am sorry I was not aware of this engagement before. However, as I am quite sure Miss Lee regards me only as a friend, no harm has been done to your cause."

" You needn't think that I am afraid of Miss Lee's preferring you to me. She is too happy in having been chosen out of a score of girls I might

have had, to fall in love with you, although you did
give yourself such a beauty-mark in her service.
Good heavens, what a fright it has made you! I am
precious glad that it was not my face that got such a
mark. I should not like to lose the reputation of
being the handsomest man in Southern Manitoba
for even my future wife."

"The reputation of being the laziest man, too,"
was the thought that involuntarily suggested itself
to Philip, as he quietly said, "That you may prove
yourself worthy of Miss Lee is my earnest wish."

"Thank you. The young lady may consider herself honored in being allied to our distinguished
family, that counts among its members some of England's nobility. What the deuce I see in her that I
should make her my wife, I hardly know. She isn't
pretty, but she is a sweet little thing. Then, too,
that's a fine property of her father's and I hear he
has quite a sum of money in the bank. As she is
the only child, she will get it all when the old chap
dies."

"Surely you are not marrying her for her property?"

"Oh, no, certainly not, but I am candid enough
to say that, much as I love her, I would think twice
before I married her or anyone else without that very
essential thing. I am no believer in 'love in a cot-
tage.'"

Philip felt as if he could not endure longer the
flippant words of his visitor, so he quietly said,
"Please excuse me, but I have my horses to look
after."

He then arose from his chair, thus politely hinting that it was time for the visitor to leave.

It was after midnight before sleep closed Philip's eyes on that wretched night. Before Pierce's visit he had hardly realized how deeply he loved Mary Lee. He felt it now to be his duty to try to quench the passion which was mastering him so completely. "Oh, God! I think I could bear to lose her did I think it would be for her advantage. But to see her marry that conceited, good-for-nothing puppy who thinks too much of himself to love any woman as a wife should be loved, is more than I can stand," was his bitter complaint.

Years passed. Philip Hastings was still a bachelor, in spite of the fact that not a few young women of the neighborhood had in a delicate way shown that he was by no means displeasing to them. He was wealthy and respected far and near as a man whose word was better than many another man's bond, but few looked upon him as a happy man. Yet he was neither a misanthrope nor an unsociable recluse. Children and dogs loved him; the unfortunate recognized in him a friend in adversity; the erring listened to his warning and advice more than the sermons of their minister, as they felt the warm sympathy of the layman much more attractive than the cold, matter-of-fact sense of duty that appeared to be the source of the latter's appeals to that better self that is to be found in the heart of every human being, no matter how degraded he may be.

# CHAPTER III.

## *LEAVING THE OLD HOME.*

HAVING succeeded in selling their Manitoba property for five thousand dollars in cash, the Pierces by the first of April were busily employed in the delightful occupation of packing. At least the wife and children were; this work was too trivial to engage the energies of so important an individual as the husand and father, who spent the greater part of his time in trying to induce some of his neighbors to follow his example.

Mrs. Pierce had not realized the strength of the ties that bound her to her home—the home to which her father had brought his little family more than twenty years ago; the home in which a loving mother had died when her only child was standing on the threshold of maidenhood; the home in which her father had breathed his last among strangers; the home which had afforded her and her family a shelter when her husband had found out that he was too clever to be appreciated by the "slow" citizens of the half dozen towns in which he had striven to obtain riches without too much hard work. In this attempt he succeeded in losing his own small capital and the much larger one of his wife's, and in involving himself in debt to such an extent that it required the greater part of his yearly allowance to pay it

on small instalments. Accordingly, having tried
the various occupations of author, land agent,
banker, grain-buyer, and storekeeper in a small
way, he had swallowed his pride and had become an ordinary farmer on the one-half of the Lee
property, his speculations having swallowed up the
other half. By this time some of the children were
old enough to help; so the family, owing largely to
the good management of the mother, had succeeded
in winning a comfortable living from the fertile acres
of their Manitoba farm.

" So you are really leaving us, and going to where
you can't see farther than a mile for the mountains.
For my part my heart is bound up in this boundless
prairie. A person has room to breathe here. I'm
sure I'd smother if I was shut up among them mountains that I hear tell of. I s'pose you'd rather I
hadn't come to see you when you're all in a bustle.
How d'ye like packing, Helen? My sakes alive!
but you have a pile of stuff," went on the loud, hearty
voice of the caller without waiting for an answer.
" It beats all how things do pile up in a few years,
and it's myself that knows it. Every time I clean
house I says to Jennie, ' I wish to goodness half
those things were out of this, I do.' But I must not
talk too long when you're so busy. I wish I could
help you but I guess I'd only be in the road and be
putting things where you'd never find them. John
always growls every time I tidy up his table, for he
says he does not know where to put his hand on a
thing then. He says he'd far rather tend to his own
table, but sakes alive! it would be an awful sight if
I was to leave the tidying to him. Men can't do

women's work, let them talk as they like. But I must really tell you what I came here for. I s'pose you don't want to take with you any more things than you really need. Now, I've heard tell that there's no winter worth speaking of where you're going. If that's the case, you'll not be needing your fur coat. I want to know if you'll sell it to me. How much do you want for it?"

"I have not thought of selling it, Mrs Moore," quietly answered Mrs. Pierce when her talkative neighbor at last gave her a chance to speak. Then, turning to her husband, who, after giving directions, sat in the only arm-chair still unpacked, reading a newspaper, "Guy, do you think I shall need my fur coat in the Okanagan?"

"Certainly not, didn't you hear Mr. Masson telling about the children going to school there bareheaded and barehanded all winter? You would look ridiculous wearing a heavy fur coat to church or out calling, while other ladies will be wearing only their summer clothes."

"But, daddy, there must be some cold weather, for Nellie Sharpe told me at school that it goes below zero sometimes," interrupted Helen, who could not bear the idea of her mother's selling her handsome fur coat.

"What does Nellie Sharpe know about it, I'd like to know."

"Her aunt lives somewhere in that valley and often writes to Nellie's mother."

"It can't be very cold where peaches can be grown. Very likely Nellie's aunt lives in the northern part of the valley, which has a much colder climate than the south. Yes, by all means sell your coat, Mary, if you can. The money will be more useful to you than the coat."

"Why don't you sell yours, then?" asked the irrepressible Helen.

"I may have to go among the mountains once in a while. Besides, a man is always more exposed to the weather than a woman, whose work lies in the shelter of a comfortable home. She is not exposed to the pitiless storms that may occasionally occur even in sunny Okanagan. But go on with your work, Helen. You are altogether too fond of talking about what does not concern you in the least," was her father's reply, spoken in a tone of rebuke.

"I wish I were a man; then perhaps people would pay more attention to what I say," thought Helen. "I do hope mamma will ask such a price that Mrs. Moore won't buy it. I don't believe all that land agent said. I noticed he took good care to tell us only about the nice things. Maybe there's more truth in what he didn't tell than in what he did tell."

But poor Helen did not get her wish, for before Mrs. Moore left she had succeeded in persuading Mrs. Pierce to sell her coat for two-thirds of its cost. And as furs had risen at least ten per cent. since the coat had been made, the visitor left feeling she had made a splendid bargain.

After three days packing, the Pierce family, the last evening of their stay in the old home, were trying to get supper with hardly anything to get it with; for they found that everything needed for that purpose had been packed. Mr. Pierce in an unusual spasm of industry had packed up all the cooking utensils, not leaving out even a knife or spoon for use on the train. Not remembering in what box he had packed the missing articles, after unpacking four huge boxes, the anxious searchers found the teapot in one, knives and forks in another, plates in another, and cups and napkins in a fourth; but at last the tired family succeeded in ferreting out enough things to obviate the necessity of dining like our first parents. But their satisfaction in this discovery was tempered by the sight of the pile of articles strewing the floor. How to get those things sorted and put back in the boxes that now seemed too small to hold one-half of them was a problem that would have to be solved by Mrs. Pierce and the children; as no more exertion could be expected from the exhausted lord and master of the household.

The last night in Manitoba was spent at Mr. Hastings', which was more convenient to the station than their old home. The housekeeper had always proved herself a friend in need to the Pierces; and now that their own home was in a dismantled condition, it required only a hint from her employer to cause her to send a hearty invitation to stay at Poplar Grove until it was time to go to the station.

"Now, Mrs. Pierce, you will be sure to write and tell us how you like your new home. We'll all miss you here, but we wish you well," said Mrs. Hicks, as she busied herself in her various duties as hostess. "What sort of house is there on the place you have bought?"

"I don't think it will do for a permanent home, but as the property costs only $3,000, we'll have two thousand to spend on buildings and other improvements."

"You have, of course, kept the property in your own name?"

"Oh, no, my husband did not think it advisable for me to be worried about business matters, and so I believe the papers are made out in his name. But, my dear Mrs. Hicks, what difference does it make? Husband and wife are one, and it seems more reasonable that all business transactions should be conducted by the husband than by the wife. Surely one's husband will do the best he can for his wife and children."

"Oh, you poor, innocent woman! Some husbands can, I suppose, but I wouldn't trust Guy Pierce to look after the interests of any other person than those of himself. It is as Mr. Hastings feared. I've heard about some queer things being done in connection with the property laws in these western provinces. After the way Pierce has mismanaged his own affairs, I don't see how Mary can be so blind," thought Mrs. Hicks, but she was too kind-hearted to arouse any suspicion of trouble in the mind of her friend, when no good would or could result.

# CHAPTER IV.

## THE NEW HOME.

AFTER a very pleasant trip, in which the magnificent mountain scenery was enjoyed to the full, our travellers arrived at Ortgeard one evening in early May. They had not found the journey wearisome, until the arrival at Sicamous, when they found themselves crowded in a dirty, small, and uncomfortable coaches on the short branch from Sicamous Junction to Okanagan Landing. The rate of travelling was snail-like, and the stops were numerous and long, and every person was glad to leave the stuffy, bad-smelling coaches for the steamer. Although the wind was cold, the sun shone brightly, and all the family spent most of their time on deck, enjoying the beautiful scenery for which this lake is so justly noted.

But it would be difficult to find any part of the Pacific Province of which the scenery could be said to be tame and uninteresting. Purple mountain ranges; snow-clad peaks kissed by the rays of the golden sun; beautiful lakes in whose smiling bosoms the sky with its fleecy clouds and the trees and rocks with all their varied hues are reflected; mountain torrents tumultuously leaping from rock to rock, the sheet of falling water looking in the distance like a bridal veil; the park-like appearance of the pine forests of the interior, through which carriages can

26

be driven where no road has ever been made; all these cause the spectator to say, " What must heaven be if earth is so beautiful !"

The Pierces were not the only ones who were fleeing from the inhospitable climate of the North-West to the " Italy of British Columbia." No fewer than seven families were on the steamer that sunny day in May, to make new homes for themselves in a more favorable clime; but our friends were the only persons bound for Ortgeard. Now, my dear readers, do not look for this place, for you will not find it on any British Columbia map.

At last our passengers were once more on terra firma, and were welcomed by no less a person than Mr. Masson himself, accompanied by his wife, who carried in her hand a large bouquet of peach blossoms, which she handed to Mrs. Pierce, as a proof of the capabilities of her new home. As their freight was not expected for a week, the Pierces went to the only hotel in the place, a rather pretentious building, but decidedly "homey," and free from the objectionable bar. In the evening Mrs. Pierce was much surprised to feel herself quite chilly in spite of a small cape she had thrown over her shoulders. When she remarked on the chilliness of the evening air, a fellow-guest said, "Oh, that's nothing unusual. I often wear my fur in the middle of the summer in the evening. You won't find many nights too warm for comfort as you would in Ontario, where I came from." Mrs. Pierce then began to wonder if she had done wisely in selling her fur coat.

In the morning the whole family went to pay a visit to their new farm. They found they had quite a bit of hill-climbing to do before they reached their destination.

"Where's the valley here? I don't see any," said Harry, as they rested for a while after having climbed a hill steeper than any of the preceding ones.

"The most of it is under the lake, I guess," said Helen.

"The best orchards are on the benches," said her father.

"The benches have very long legs," replied Helen.

"I am glad, mother, our horses are on the way. I am afraid you would not get to church often if you had to climb this hill on foot."

"I may get used to climbing hills after a while," said her mother with a rather tired smile.

"How are we going to stow all our furniture in that shack, I wonder ?" were Helen's first words when she saw the frame "lean-to" which was the only building on the place.

Well might she ask the question, as the shack boasted of only two small rooms, the dimensions of the whole building being only sixteen feet by eighteen.

"We'll get a tent for sleeping, so we can manage until the house is built," said Mr. Pierce, encouragingly, although he could not help feeling that perhaps it was not always wise to buy simply on hearsay. This feeling was strengthened when he and the children inspected the orchard, while Mrs. Pierce, being too tired to do any more climbing, sat on a large stone that lay conveniently near the shack. They had not gone far into the orchard before they discovered that many of the trees were badly broken down.

"Humph!" said Mr. Pierce, "this looks as if cattle had been in. Some of these trees are utterly ruined."

"Aren't the peach trees lovely, though, dad? And, oh! just look at those trees that are all white with blossom. What are they, apple trees?" asked Harry, to whom any kind of fruit tree was a great curiosity.

"No, they can't be apple trees. It is too early for them. They may be cherry. Let us go to see."

Mr. Pierce was found to be right, when the explorers arrived at the trees that had attracted Harry's attention.

Half an hour passed before Mrs. Pierce saw the rest of the family. They could hardly believe that they had been away from her so long, when she told them she had begun to wonder if anything had happened.

"What do you think of the orchard, Guy?" was the rather anxious question.

"It's not too bad. The prospects are good for a fine crop of peaches, plums and cherries. The apple trees are too young to bear much yet, I suppose. You ought to be well rested by this time, Mary. Come, let us be going back to the hotel."

But they were not to get away from their future home so soon. A tall, lanky, lantern-jawed man with shrewd eyes and a grizzly goatee, who had been leaning on the boundary fence for the last ten minutes, was now seen rapidly crossing the intervening space between the fence and the shack.

"I reckon you must be my new neighbors, the Pierces from Manitoba. My name is Newman, and I own the next ranch. That's my house yonder," said the stranger, pointing to a pretty bungalow a

few rods to the north. "My wife and I will be
mighty glad to have neighors so handy. Just come
over whenever you feel like it. We'll always be glad
to see you. Is this your eldest daughter? A fine,
healthy-looking girl, just the age of my Susan, I
reckon. What may your name be, my dear?"

"Helen, sir," the answer was hurriedly given, in
the fear that the neighbor might not give much
chance for it to be given.

"Helen, after Helen of Troy? Let us hope that
you'll not make as much mischief as she did. Well,
neighbor, what do you think of your purchase?"

"There are some very fine trees on the place," was
the non-committal answer given in a cool tone, as
Mr. Pierce did not altogether like the free-and-easy
manner of his inquisitive neighbor. But the kindly
twinkle in the sharp eyes rather attracted his wife.

"You ought to see mine, if you think those are
fine. They were planted the same year. You can
see them from here. Now, what do you think of
them?" proudly asked Mr. Newman, as he fondly
gazed at his cherished trees.

"You don't mean to say that those trees are the
same age as ours! Why should they be so much
larger?" asked Mrs. Pierce. "Is the soil so much
better?"

"No, the difference is not in the soil, but in the
work. The company looked after this place, but I
looked after my own. Every tree on my place has
been planted by my own hands, and I have spared
neither time nor trouble in looking after them. I
tell you, Mrs. Pierce, that if you want a good orchard
you must look after things yourself, and not have

every Tom, Dick or Harry fooling with them. Take the pruning, for example; the company engaged a pruner who posed as an expert. He pruned the trees according to his idea, which, in his own view, was the only correct one. Then next year comes along another expert, who says the first man spoilt the trees, so he prunes them according to his idea, which, of course, is also the only right one; so the poor trees don't know how they are expected to grow. Now, I have made up my mind how I want my trees to grow, and I prune them so they'll grow that way, and I'd like to see the man or woman who could make me change it. I don't say that my way of pruning is the best, but it suits me; and what's better, it suits the trees, too. Then there's the irrigating. I water my trees whenever they need it; but the company trees are irrigated whenever it suits the convenience of the men. But I'm afraid I've talked too long. I suppose you are staying at the hotel. A nice, homelike place that! Pretty hard to beat in a little place like Ortgeard! We don't allow any drunks around it, either. I hope you will like it here. Don't expect too much, then you won't be disappointed. I don't say land-agents lie, but they generally show only one side of the picture. But I must really go now; good-bye." So saying, the long-legged and long-winded farmer rapidly returned home.

## CHAPTER V.

### THE OTHER SIDE OF THE PICTURE.

MAY had passed away and glorious June had come, shedding golden sunshine over hill and dale, over mountain and lake, throughout the fair Okanagan Valley.

The Pierces had moved into their new home after waiting at the hotel more than two weeks for their freight. During the stay at the hotel Mr. Pierce was presented with the bill for pruning and spraying, which took him by surprise. He now began to find that a little amount of work in the Pacific Province costs a great amount of money. Then, to make matters worse, he was told by Mr. Newman that the spraying would probably be of little use, as most of the work had been done during windy weather.

Near the shanty had been put up a large tent, which served for sleeping accommodations for the whole family, chintz curtains serving the purpose of partitions. A stable was built for the horses, and men were busy working at the foundation of the new house. They did not have far to go for stones for that purpose, as there were plenty on the lot, especially on the uncultivated portion. In fact, any person would be welcome to all the stones he wanted, for there would still be plenty left.

In Manitoba the expense of keeping horses had not been considered at all; but here it became a rather serious question as to whether or not it would pay to keep them when hay and oats were so dear.

The whole family found the hot weather very trying, but the pleasant evenings always afforded a grateful relief. Dust, heat and sand-flies were forgotten while sitting in front of the house enjoying the refreshing breeze and watching the ever-changing surface of the lake—sapphire, emerald, vermilion, all seemed to be struggling for mastery of color on its glassy waters; not that the lake was always calm. Far from it; calm it might be one hour, and the next lashed into fury by variable Erebus' messengers that had been suddenly released from their bonds in some mountain gorge. All the troubles of the day were forgotten in that peaceful hour of rest when it was too dark to work and too soon to light the lamp. At least so Mrs. Pierce said, and all the rest of the family were quite willing to agree with her. At such a time the most industrious person is easily satisfied with any excuse for doing nothing.

Mrs. Pierce, aided by Helen and Harry, when they could spare time from their school duties, had spent a great deal of time in making a garden, but no sooner did the cucumbers, melons and other plants come up than they suddenly, like Jonah's gourd, wilted away in a night.

"Whatever can be the matter with the things?" asked Helen of her mother at last in despair.

"I suppose it is the cutworms. I thought from what Mr. Masson said that we would be free from

3

all pests here. But I fear he showed us only one side of the picture. We are now seeing the other. We'll have to use bran and Paris green as we used to do in Manitoba. I wish they would eat up the weeds that grow so fast here. I believe that they grow faster here than in Manitoba."

"Well, other people can grow vegetables here, and fine ones, too; so I am sure we can, also. All we have to do is to fight the pests for a week or two, then their season will be over. Newman's have a splendid garden; their tomatoes are in blossom already."

"Yes, I know. They grew their own plants, but, of course, we were not here in time to do that. We shall be able to manage better next year, I hope," said Mrs. Pierce in a more cheerful tone. "But here come your father and Harry in to dinner, and the table is not laid yet; so we must hurry in."

A look at her husband's face showed the anxious wife that things had not gone smoothly with him that morning.

"We are early in, I know; but I thought we might as well come in and rest as stand out in the broiling sun trying to irrigate with a miserable dribble of water," was the husband's reason for his premature arrival.

"Isn't there water enough?" asked Helen.

"Yes, for some people, but we don't happen to be the lucky ones. By the time those at the upper end take all they want, there's precious little left for us at this lower end. It's the most miserable system, or rather want of system, I ever saw in my life. There's enough water leaking out of the company's flumes

to water four or five ten-acre lots.   Then there are
some people here who don't think there's anything
wrong in stealing their neighbor's supply of water."

"Why don't you complain to Mr. Jenkins?" asked
Mrs. Pierce.

"I have, but he says he can't be at half a dozen
places at the same time.   Just as soon as his back is
turned some of these water thieves come along, pull
out their gates or put in some stones in the main
flume and thus turn aside the water that should come
down to us into their own place.   Such mean rascals
should be punished, I say."

No sooner were these angry words uttered than
May came running in with wide-open eyes and
mouth, panting from her eager haste to reach the
house.

"Oh, dad, the water is breaking out of the ditches
and running all over the orchard!   It's making big
holes in the ground, too!" she said, as soon as she
could find breath.

With an angry curse the discouraged rancher,
accompanied by Harry, rushed out of the house.   The
news was true.   The water-thieves had evidently
secured all they wanted for the time, and had now
kindly turned on the full supply of water to refresh
their less fortunate neighbor's orchard.   Had Mr.
Pierce been at his post all would have been well, but
as he had deserted it in disgust, his ditches were now
broken out and the freed water was wandering at its
own sweet will, doing more harm than good.   More
than two hours passed before Mr. Pierce and Harry
could leave the water to go in to their dinner.   To

say that the former was cross is putting it very mildly.

"If I had hold of Masson to-day I'd punch his head for him. What fools we were to swallow all he said as if it were gospel truth! One would think to hear him talk that all one had to do on a fruit-farm was to pick fruit and to eat it. I never worked so hard in my life before as I have done since I came here, and I can't see what I've done after all. If I'd only come out here first I'd never have bought land where the company used leaky wooden flumes to convey the water to the different ranches. Mr. Rowe was telling me of a new place, just twelve miles from here, where the pipe system is used. Now, that's something like the thing; there's no water wasted by leakage or evaporation; one can have water for domestic use in winter as well as summer if he chooses to pay a little extra; and those at the tail have as good a show as at the head. I'd sell this place to-morrow for what I paid for it and buy there if I could."

"If our place were flumed the same as Mr. Newman's, there would not be so much trouble irrigating," said Helen.

"Will you ever be tired quoting Mr. Newman?" was her father's peevish reply. "It's 'Mr. Newman does this,' and Mr. Newman's trees, and Mr. Newman's methods, until I declare I'm sick of hearing his name. Where's the money coming from, I'd like to know, to build flumes? By the time those carpenters get through building the house there'll be precious little left of the money we got from the sale of the Manitoba farm and stock."

However, after enjoying a plentiful supply of well-cooked provisions and some delicious cherries off his own trees, Mr. Pierce began to see that the other side of the picture was not so dark after all. How true it is that a good meal has a wonderful effect upon our view of things, especially a man's!

# CHAPTER VI.

## HELEN'S PERPLEXITY.

HELEN and Harry had been attending school regularly ever since their arrival in Ortgeard. As the former had been one of the most promising pupils in the Manitoba school, she found no difficulty in being assigned a place in the entrance class; but well-up as she was in general subjects, she discovered that she would have little enough time to prepare for the coming examination in literature and British Columbia history and geography, as the former was different from what she had been studying in the East, and the latter she had not studied.

Susan Newman was in the same class, so the friendship of the two girls was further increased by this common interest. They used to take turns in spending the evenings at each other's home, reviewing together the next day's work.

One evening after Helen had been going to school nearly a month, she happened to say to Susan, "I have now only a month to get up all my work for the entrance. Do you think, Sue, that I'll manage it? I've had to review so much of the work by myself, as the class had gone over most of it before I came. What I study by myself I can't remember nearly as well as that which I've taken in the class."

" I think you would beat all the rest of us if you only had that month; but, my dear girl, I am afraid you can't count upon a month."

" Why, what do you mean? It's nearly a month to the last of June. We generally have the entrance examination in Manitoba the last week in June."

" But this isn't Manitoba. The examination may be in two weeks' time, or three weeks', or worse still, next week, for all I know. Last year it was here the second week in May. My! what a rush the poor youngsters had to get over the work in time! But I guess it was harder on the teacher than on the pupils. There was one blessing about the affair, though; the members of the class—at least the most of them— took their revenge by leaving school for the holidays as soon as it was over."

" But I don't understand what you mean the least bit!" said Helen, in a tone of anxiety and surprise. " Do you mean to say that Mr. Turner doesn't know himself when the examination will be?"

" Yes, I do mean just that. If he knew he would tell us, but he hasn't got word yet."

" Why can't the examinations be held at the same time all over the province, the same as in other places?"

" The inspector can't be at half a dozen places at the same time, can he?"

" No, I don't suppose he can. But it is not necessary for him to preside at all of them, is it? Couldn't the teachers exchange schools, or couldn't some other qualified persons be found to preside at each place?"

"Cost too much, Helen. At least your last suggestion would, and I suppose the department is afraid the teachers might make too easy-going examiners."

"It does not seem to me to be a fair arrangement. Why, some schools have three or four weeks longer to prepare than the others."

"Yes, that is true; but what is the use in finding fault with the powers that be?"

"All I can say is that if I have to be ready in two weeks I may as well give up the idea of writing this year. I have planned my work for a month at least, and mother will not allow me to sit up any later than I have been doing."

"Now, Helen, you must not back out of writing like this. Mr. Turner won't let you, anyway. I am pretty sure he counts upon you for one of the sure ones. Get up earlier in the morning."

"I can't do that either, at least to study. Mother says that I must not study more than two hours a day besides what I do at school."

"You could study an hour or so in the morning without your mother's knowing it."

"I could, but I won't. I think too much of my mother to disobey her, and too much of myself to stoop to deception," was Helen's indignant answer.

"Well, you don't need to be so huffy about it! I didn't mean any harm," said Susan, as Helen turned to open the gate.

It was a very sad-faced girl, indeed, that went to her room that night, and truth compels me to say that she shed quite a few tears before sleep closed her eyelids.

The next day, as Mr. Turner assured her that her chances of success were as good as any of the other members of her class, Helen pursued her studies with renewed vigor, especially as she now knew that the examination would take place in two weeks.

The time passed swiftly away, too swiftly the anxious candidates for entrance honors thought. Two days more and they were to be permitted to relieve their wearied brains by putting their knowledge, whether little or great, on numerous sheets of paper.

The two friends were walking slowly home when Susan, after looking carefully around to see that none of the rest of the scholars were near, turned to Helen, saying, " Can you keep a secret ?"

" I don't know that I ever tried to. Why ?"

" Well, are you well up in Australia ? Can you draw a map of it well ?"

" Not very. I have been spending so much of my time lately studying British Columbia, but I intend to review the British Empire before Thursday."

" I advise you to do so; also to find out who are the premiers of Great Britain, New Zealand and British Columbia, if you don't know now. Be able to tell all about the North-West Rebellion and the Alaska Boundary question. Oh, yes, and in arithmetic be sure that you know how many litres there are in a decalitre."

" I know that now, but I don't know who the premier of New Zealand is. It doesn't tell us that in the history."

" Neither does it tell us the present premier of British Columbia or of Great Britain; yet you know them, don't you?"

" The teacher told us them; then I've often heard my father talking of the British premier, so I couldn't help remembering him, anyway. I don't think we should be expected to know all the premiers in the British Empire, though. I don't believe the examiners themselves know all of them. But why do you say I should pay particular attention to all those things you mentioned? Are those favorite questions of the British Columbia examiners?"

" I don't know whether they are favorite questions or not, but I have a friend not a hundred miles away who was kind enough to telephone me some of the questions that are on the rural papers. At first I thought I would keep the information to myself. But I thought afterwards that that would be mean, so I'm telling you. Why do you look so horrified? One would think that I was telling you to kill some-body!"

" I would far rather you had said nothing to me about these questions. It isn't fair or honorable to try to find out what the questions are before we are given the papers."

" Maybe it isn't right to try to find out, but I didn't do that; but when I have a friend good-natured enough to tell me a few things through the telephone, I'm not going to be fool enough not to make use of the information so kindly given."

" What would the Education Department say if they knew that such things were done?"

" Oh, I don't know or care either. I don't think they'd say much. Why should they when they give such splendid chances for information to be given?"

" I suppose they rely upon the honor of the pupils," said Helen, quietly. " But here is our gate, good night."

" Oh, dear, how I wish Susan hadn't told me those questions! I intended to study Australia to-night, anyway. It's easy to draw. I don't know much about the North-West Rebellion, so how can I help, when I review the last part of the Canadian history, paying particular attention to that and the Alaska Boundary question, now I know they are going to be asked? But it does not seem right to make use of this information. But am I making use of it, when very likely I should have looked up those things, anyway?" Thus the evil and the good struggled for conquest in the heart of this young girl, who hitherto had shrunk from dishonesty in any guise, as the leaves of the sensitive plant shrink from the touch of the human hand.

Mr. Pierce and the younger children had gone to bed, leaving the mother and Helen to go on with their work.

" Why that sigh, my dear girl? I think it would be better for you to rest. You look too tired to study any more to-night. You know there is such a thing as over-taxing the brain."

" It is not study that is worrying me to-night, mother. It is something else."

" What is troubling you, my dear? Tell me, per-haps I can help you."

It was not many minutes before the mother was informed of all that had passed between her daughter and Susan Newman. She sat for a few minutes in deep thought.

"Have you looked up any of those questions since Susan told you, Helen?"

"Yes, mother, but I think I should have looked them up, anyway."

"But not so carefully as you did? Think before you speak, dear!"

"I am afraid not," was the answer, frankly given.

"You must not write on this examination at all, Helen!"

"Oh, mother, after all my studying! Mr. Turner will be angry if I do not write."

"The studying should benefit you whether you write or not. You cannot touch pitch without being soiled, neither can you do anything in which there is the slightest taint of dishonor without a stain upon your soul. I want my Helen to grow up a noble woman, free from any suspicion of falsehood or dishonor. Character is of more importance than passing examinations. Do you not agree with me, Helen?"

"Yes, mother, but I have been thinking that I might write at Vernon on the urban papers. They are not the same as the rural, and nobody knows the questions on those papers except the men who made them up."

"When is that examination?"

"The last week in June, I think."

" It will cost something to send you there and to pay your board. But I wish to go there to get some furniture, and I may as well go then as later. You will have a little longer to study, and it will all be for the best; so cheer up, Helen."

" You don't know how much better I feel, mother. I am so glad I told you everything. I hope I shall never have any secrets from you."

" I hope not, dear. But it is your bedtime now, so good night!"

" I wonder why the British Columbia Education Department places temptation in the way of our children by having the entrance examinations at different dates instead of having all at the same time?" thought Mrs. Pierce, as she retired to rest. Other people wonder why, too.

In spite of the protestations of her teacher and fellow-pupils, Helen wrote on the urban papers. When the results of the examination were published, she had the satisfaction of knowing that she had passed with more marks than her fellow-pupils, and that every one was honestly earned.

## CHAPTER VII.

### QUEER MISS TODD.

It was a beautiful day in July—not too hot, as there was a pleasant breeze blowing from the lake, which tempered the otherwise hot air. The younger children had all gone down to the lake to play, Mr. Pierce had gone to the coast on business, and his wife and Helen were sitting on the little stoop in front of the shack, when their attention was drawn to a horse and rig which stopped at their gate. The rig's only occupant was a very tall and rather stout woman, who nimbly jumped out of the vehicle, and tied the horse before Helen could get half the distance down the path on her way to help her.

"My! Mother Nature was exceedingly generous when she made you," said Helen to herself, as she looked at the visitor. Nearly six feet in height, which was increased to the extent of an additional six inches by a hat with a very high crown, and stout in proportion, her size was certainly not to be despised. Her short dress disclosed a pair of feet clad in number eight shoes, and her large, brawny hands were uncovered by any gloves—not because the lady did not own them, as she carried a pair of men's kid gloves in her left hand. These she now put on when she saw the young girl coming down the hill to meet her. Her nose might have been

called Roman, but it was as generous in proportion
as the rest of her person; her cheek bones were high,
and her mouth was very large, its beauty not being
increased by two prominent teeth in the upper jaw
and by a decidedly conspicuous mustache on the
upper lip. The square lower jaw showed firmness,
and the bright, piercing eyes showed keen observation. Although most persons would have called her
ugly, when Helen looked in her face as she greeted
her, she was attracted rather than repelled. The
stranger's hand-clasp was no cold, fashionable touch-
ing of the finger-tips, but a warm, friendly pressure.

"This is Helen Pierce, I suppose. I have heard
my niece, Ida, speak of you very often. My name
is Todd—Miss Todd, not Mrs., thank heaven! And
how is your mother, my dear? I needn't ask, as I
see her sitting on the stoop. What a hill this is to
climb! I see you are building your new house
nearer the road. A very sensible thing to do, unless
you want to shorten your days!"

By this time Helen and Miss Todd had arrived
at the shack. Helen introduced the visitor to her
mother, and then opened the door to admit her into
the room which served so many purposes.

"Let me sit here, please; the stoop was good
enough for you before I came to bother you, so I
guess it's good enough for me. Give me a chair—a
good, strong one—not one of your flimsy ones, for
I'm no light-weight, I can tell you. But I don't need
to tell you that. You have only to look at me to
know that much. But I don't complain of my
looks; I am as my Creator made me, and since He is
satisfied, I am."

"Sometimes it is an advantage to be big," said Mrs. Pierce, as her visitor sat down in the substantial arm-chair brought out by Helen.

"Yes, you are quite right about that, especially when a person has to be man and woman both on a fruit-ranch. You must excuse my not calling upon you before, but I really could not get away until the school closed, so that Ida could take care of the baby. I suppose you know I have quite a family to look after. You wouldn't be here this long without hearing what an 'old fool' I have been."

"Not an 'old fool' by any means, but a dear, kind-hearted, unselfish woman, to take all those children into your home and big heart!" exclaimed Helen, looking as if she wanted to kiss the giantess.

"Thank you for your good opinion of me. But I am sorry to tell you that it is quite undeserved, for you see before you a big bundle of selfishness. I was afraid my conscience would not give me a moment's peace if I did not mother those helpless children. Then, too, did I not think of the help they would be to me in my old age? So you see that selfishness was at the bottom of it all. Talk about pagans! I think the most of us are idolaters whose chief idol is self! But I am talking nonsense and showing my selfishness by trying to think I am no worse than others."

"Would you mind telling me about your taking the children? I heard something about it from the Newmans, but not any particulars. They are your sister's, are they not? But don't tell me if the story is too painful for you to give," said Mrs. Pierce in a gentle tone.

"Yes, I'll tell you. I only wish that every woman in British Columbia could hear the story. My sister was not much like me; she was only of average height and quite a beauty. When she was only eighteen she married a young fellow whose father and mother lived on a farm not very far from New Westminster. He came to this valley on a prospecting tour, and stayed at our place for some time. It appeared to be a case of love at first sight with both of the young people. Before he left he asked my father for Grace's hand in marriage. After having written to his home for particulars my father consented. A favorable account having been given, the marriage took place shortly after the first meeting. As father was a just man he treated his children all alike, so when Grace married he gave her a thousand dollars to help her husband buy a forty-acre farm near his father's that happened to be for sale. For a year or two the young couple appeared to be doing nicely. Jack, I mean my brother-in-law, had been given a good start, as his father had helped him liberally, so that he started in life with a good, farm, stock, and all the necessary machinery without a cent of debt on any of it.

"But it was only seeming after all. A cloud was beginning to darken my sister's home, although her cheerful letters led us to believe that she was as happy as any woman could wish to be. Before five years had passed away a letter came to my father from Jack appealing for assistance on account of bad crops and poor prices. Before giving any more assistance father thought it wiser to go and see for himself how matters stood. So, although he hated travelling and could not well spare the time, he went to Riverholm. Although Jack did his best to hide the true facts of the case, he could not escape the sharp eyes of my father, who found, to his great grief, that not poor crops—not poor prices—but drink and gambling were the causes of his son-in-law's bad luck. He had managed to keep his fondness for both a secret from us all before his marriage, and I will give him the credit of believing he would be man enough to conquer these vices for the sake of his wife. But he found—as too many have—that it is far easier to go down hill than up, and that good resolutions are easy to make but mighty hard to put into action. My father made him a proposal, which was this: 'You put your property in your wife's name—she paid for nearly the half of it anyway—and for the sake of her and the children I shall pay all your debts, although it will cripple me very much.' Jack was indignant at this offer. 'I'm not a baby who can't manage my own affairs. If those are your terms, keep your money to yourself.' Then father begged Grace to come home with the children. But she would not listen to such a proposal. She had married Jack for better or for worse, she said, and she would not leave him until he insisted on her doing so. When he heard that father wanted to take her and the children home he said, 'If you want to send me to hell, then take my wife and children away.' I do really think the poor fellow loved his family, but his love for them was not strong enough to choke the snake that was slowly but surely winding around him, paralyzing in him all that was good and noble.

"But I must hasten to the end. Things went from bad to worse, until my brother-in-law, after having heavily mortgaged his property, shot himself one never-to-be-forgotten day last winter. It needed only this to kill my sister, who did not live a month after her husband's death. As soon as I heard of my brother-in-law's death I went to see Grace, whom I knew to be very ill. I am glad to say that father had passed away before the suicide had taken place. Before Grace's death her father-in-law and I tried to save something from the wreck, but it was impossible. Everything was in his name, and everything went to pay his debts, incurred mostly in gambling and for liquor; nothing was left for the innocent children and the broken-hearted wife who had sacrificed her life in her efforts to keep the wolf from the door. Is it right, is it just, that our Western married women should work their fingers to the bone in their efforts to help their husbands in building homes only to find that they have no legal right to those same homes, to find that their husbands may, if they feel like it, mortgage everything, or even will all away from them without any redress?

"My sister's is not the only case; I know of others. I was born in this province, not very far from Vancouver. In my childhood there was no Vancouver, and the C.P.R. had not yet been built to link together the distant East and the far-off, unknown West. The hardships of the settler were then far greater than they are now. Our nearest neighbors were a family consisting of father, mother and three children—two strong boys and one girl troubled with a lame knee. They were all hard-

working, but they possessed none of the luxuries and
few of the necessities of life, as the husband and
father was a miser. Work! work! from morn till
night was the order of the day. The wife and mother
had to help log and stump all day, then do the house-
work and sewing, while her husband and master lay
comfortably snoozing away in bed. Her lame
daughter did what she could inside while the rest
were out, although her knee often caused her such
intense pain that she had to lie down to rest.
But her father's step outside was always a signal for
her to rise and go on with her work, for she could
stand the pain better than the taunts of her cruel
father. After a few years' hard work life with them
began to be more comfortable. The farm was a good
one, and having been well worked was counted one
of the best in our neighborhood. But who had made
it such? Not the father and sons alone, but also the
wife and daughter. Did the latter reap the fruit of
their labor? No! Just when life was beginning to
get a little easier on the farm the father died leaving the farm, stock and everything else to the two
sons; the paltry sum of a hundred dollars to his
daughter and nothing at all to his wife. Some people
said it was a shame, but others said that the boys
would be sure to do the right thing by their mother
and sister. But did they do it? Not a bit of it!
At the time of the father's death the eldest son was
married but living at home. Both he and his wife
soon made things so unpleasant that the two un-
fortunates had to leave. The poor girl tried to make
a living for her mother and herself by sewing, but
never very strong, she soon had to be taken to the

hospital, where she soon died. The mother ended her days in the Old Ladies' Home.

"Now, my dear Mrs. Pierce, you may think me an impertinent busy-body, but I really think for your children's sake, if not for your own, that you should see that you have some legal claim to this property."

This advice was not given in the presence of Helen, who had gone into get supper ready.

"But my husband is neither a gambler nor a drunkard. Surely I can trust him to do the best he can for us all," said Mrs. Pierce, indignantly, although an unbidden thought told her, "Does not your past experience tell you that his best is very unsatisfactory? Your money bought this place, therefore you should have it in your own name."

"Now, dearie, don't be offended at what an old maid says; I am always 'putting my foot in it,' as the saying is, but I have given my warning, whether wisely or not. I must go now, as it is getting late. Do come to see me soon, and make up your mind to spend the whole afternoon with me. Bring the children along, they'll find plenty of playmates. No, thank you, Helen, I can't stay this time for supper; I'll just take a cup of tea out here and then I must go, for I see Ginger is getting quite impatient. I shall expect the whole family to Canyon Ranch. That's the name of my place."

While chatting over the tea Mrs. Pierce discovered that Miss Todd had not been to church since she had assumed the responsibility of raising a family.

"You must not think me a heathen, but the baby has not been well until lately, at least not well enough to trust him to anyone else. I don't think I have any right to disturb other people by a cross baby. I know some of the people of my church think I am getting careless and worldly, but my Heavenly Father knows the reasons. I talked to Him about it and He said: 'Don't worry. I know you are not forgetting Me.' As long as He is satisfied I don't care what people say. They call me 'Queer Miss Todd,' and 'Queer Miss Todd' I shall be to the end of my days."

"She may be queer, mother, but I think the world would be better if there were a few more people like her," said Helen after the visitor had departed.

# CHAPTER VIII.

## *A VISIT TO CANYON RANCH.*

ONE fine afternoon in the latter end of July a rig, in which were seated all the Pierces, was moving rapidly along the lake shore road. It was a very pleasant drive. To the right lay the lake, which was in one of its peaceful, sunny moods, mirroring in its glassy bosom the blue sky dotted here and there with sleepy, fleecy clouds; to the left, followed in rapid succession flourishing ten-acre ranches, smaller five-acre ones, then smaller ones still; on all of which could be seen peach trees loaded with fruit crimsoning and yellowing in the warm rays of the summer sun; late cherry trees full of luscious fruit —some purple black, others a dark red; and apple trees, whose branches were beginning to bend with the treasure of Hesperides gradually coloring for the coming harvest. Next came the little village of Ortgeard, nestled in a long but narrow valley, sheltered to a great extent from all winds but the east by the protecting arms of the mountain range that, after the village was left, came nearly to the water's edge. After leaving the village the road ascended for a short distance a small shoulder of the ridge, then went down again into what might be called a continuation of the same valley, as the hill was not high enough to be considered a divide.

The farm buildings of Canyon Ranch appeared in
sight shortly after the travellers passed a bridge
over the creek that distributed its waters to half of
the farms in the vicinity of Ortgeard.  Canyon
Ranch was the first of several prosperous ranches in
this part of the valley, which here widened to the
breadth of from two to three miles, this width con-
tinuing for a distance of several miles.

"What a lovely place!  After all, this is a beautiful country to live in," said Mrs. Pierce, as this
prosperous expanse of fruit-growing land burst into
view.

"We have here the oldest fruit-ranches in the district," said Mr. Pierce.  "That is one reason why I
took my valuable time to drive you and the children
to an old maid's ranch.  If anything worth while
can be made here out of fruit-growing, these old
ranchers ought to know.  While you are making your
visit at Miss Todd's, I shall visit some of these pros-
perous-looking ranches, and try to find out some
things that may be of use to me."

After a good deal of persuasion on the part of
Miss Todd, Mr. Pierce put the horses into the stable.

"Now I have you here, I mean to keep you until
the cool of the evening, so all take off your things
and stay for tea," said Miss Todd, her face glowing
with hospitable fervor.  "I want to take you all over
my little ranch and to have a good talk."

"Well, I shall accept your kind invitation for
myself and family if you will not mind my leaving
you for two or three hours, as I wish to inspect some
of your neighbors' ranches.  This place seems to be
quite a 'Garden of Eden,' of which I see before me

the Eve," said Mr. Pierce, gazing admiringly at his surroundings.

"Where is the Adam?" asked Miss Todd with a smile.

"He is hiding somewhere," was the smiling rejoinder.

Well might Mr. Pierce call Canyon Ranch the "Garden of Eden." The verandah in front of the low farmhouse was well screened from public gaze by crimson ramblers, alternating with climbing white roses; in front of the house there lay a lawn, whose velvety smoothness and pleasing verdure was certainly very refreshing to the eye. A well-kept gravel path divided the lawn into two parts; on each side of the path were flower-beds, in which were to be found some rare flowers, as well as the old-fashioned favorites. Along the garden fence were beds devoted to tulips, crocuses and hyacinths in the early spring; lilies in the early summer, and gladioli and dahlias in the late summer and fall. At the time of the Pierces' visit the air was sweet with the fragrance of many different varieties of lilies that proved the fertility of the soil by showing their heads above the top of the fence. At the back of the house was the vegetable and small fruit garden; in this were to be found some of the more common varieties of flowers—those that our forefathers loved. On each side of the house shrubbery shut off the view of the kitchen-garden from the lawn.

The house itself was of modest size, being only a story and a half in height, and having on the ground floor a living-room, dining-room, bedroom, kitchen and pantry. From the dining-room broad stairs led to the two large bedrooms upstairs. All the rooms were well-lighted, especially the kitchen, which was really the sunniest and most cheerful room in the house. Nothing seemed to be for mere show, but everything for comfort.

"What a homey place," said Helen to herself as she entered the cheerful living-room. " No disagreeable, musty smell here!"

"You evidently believe in letting plenty of sunlight into your best room. Are you not afraid of getting your carpet faded?" said Mrs. Pierce, as she sat down in the comfortable arm-chair which Miss Todd had given her.

"I can buy new carpets, but not health; the sun is a good doctor," was the short but pithy answer.

"Now, dearies, I think I'll send you into the orchard to see if you can find any ripe peaches to eat. All the children, except the baby, are there, and your mother and I shall come out when it gets cooler. There's the baby crying. I must go and get him."

She soon re-entered the room carrying in her arms a curly-headed little boy about a year old. Seeing a stranger in the room the shy little fellow turned aside his face, resting his head on his aunt's expansive breast. In a little while the visitor was able to entice the little one to her lap, thus relieving Miss Todd of her charge.

Before two hours passed away Mr. Pierce made his appearance, and all went to visit the orchard. In the vegetable garden were a few rows of trees of different varieties. The rows were so far apart that there was plenty of space available for all the vegetables required for family use.

"I see you have all kinds of trees here. Do you think, Miss Todd, that is a good plan?" asked Mr. Pierce.

"No, I don't, at least not for a commercial orchard. These trees are intended for our own use. The commercial orchard is farther on," so saying, Miss Todd led the way to a scene of beauty and profit. First they came to the peach-orchard; not a weed was to be seen; no flower-garden could have had better pulverized soil; the trees were all of uniform height, with the exception of some young trees that had taken the place of dead ones; in some rows the trees were laden with fragrant gold and crimson peaches, in others the peaches were just beginning to color and were evidently not full grown.

"I believe in having my early varieties all together and the later ones by themselves, as the water has to be put on to suit the different times of ripening; but I have a few early ones among the later varieties, as those trees were not true to name. One of the most annoying things with which we fruit-growers have to contend is the dishonesty or carelessness of nurserymen. When our trees are not true to name, our carefully-planned orchard looks as if chance had had its own way, and we are criticized for our lack of brain when it is lack of honor that is at fault. You will not find any peaches in this orchard fit to eat, as we have to pick them for shipping purposes before they are really ripe, at least ripe enough to eat. I pride myself on having very few culls. When a person is used to it he can tell when a peach is fit to pick without feeling it, which is bad for the peach and slow for the picker. Now come to my apple orchard."

Here the trees were planted much farther apart than were the peach trees. Care had evidently been taken to have the same varieties together, but here also nurserymen had done their best to spoil the plan.

"How many varieties have you?" asked Mrs. Pierce.

"Only four here, Newton Pippin, Spitzenberg, Wagner and Wealthy. I have about a dozen varieties in the house orchard, as apples are my favorite fruit and I like to have some all the year round."

"You are not treating your apple trees the same as your peach," said Mr. Pierce; "you are allowing the clover to grow among them."

"Yes, the trees are so large now that I do not cultivate much among them; but I cut only one crop of hay, the rest is cut and allowed to lie on the land. Once in a while the clover is ploughed down, but I always sow it again the same season. I have had clover sown this season in the peach orchard, too, for a cover crop for winter. I shall have it ploughed down early next spring."

"Do the trees then need protection for winter? I did not think the frost was severe enough to hurt them in this ' Italy of British Columbia.' "

"Neither it is, Mrs. Pierce, as a rule; but there are exceptional winters here as in other places, and it is a good thing to be prepared for the worst. I suppose you noticed a part of the peach orchard where most of the trees were much younger than the others?"

" Yes."

" Well, one winter we had very little snow, and
there came an exceptionally severe frost that killed
a great many trees, both mine and those of my neighbors. Never having had such a frost before, few of
us had taken any precautions, so many of us lost
heavily. It was the first year after my father's
death, and I had been planning to devote one-fifth
of my peach crop to missions. For a long time I
thought the trees would come round all right.
' Surely,' thought I, ' God will not be so cruel as to
allow my beautiful trees to be killed, especially when
I intend making such a good use of them!' But the
warm weather in June soon revealed the fact that the
peach trees, and also many of the cherry trees, were
a total loss. I felt then as if I could sympathize
with Job's wife when she told her husband to ' curse
God and die.' Don't look so horrified, Mrs. Pierce,
I am afraid you think I am a wicked woman. Well,
I was then, I am afraid; but to tell the truth, don't
the best of us sometimes have quite a bit of the old
Adam in us? I am a long time learning my lesson,
but I think I see what the Lord intended to teach
me by allowing this misfortune to come."

" What's the lesson, please?" asked Mrs. Pierce
in a soft voice.

" It is, I think, that He would rather have ourselves than our gifts. I was getting too fond of the
trees. A person does almost worship the things that
he has worked so much among, especially flowers and
fruit trees. I suppose you think me very childish;
but sometimes I feel as if the trees and flowers were
talking to me. I can't bear to see even a pine tree

cut down. It seems to me as if it could feel pain, as if there were indeed living in every tree a spirit, as our heathen ancestors taught. But I am wandering from my subject. To go on with the lesson, God does not wish us to forget the Creator in our love of the created. He can do without us or our help. When He chooses to make use of us, it is because we are helped thereby to become better fitted for His service. As the blind poet so beautifully expressed it, ' They also serve who only stand and wait.' I had begun to think I was paying God quite a compliment by giving Him one-fifth of what He had given me."

" Don't you think, then, we should give at least the tenth?"

" Yes, I do; but to give ourselves is the most important thing. If we really do that we shall not think that, after having given the tenth or the fifth, we have a right to do what we like with the rest. We are accountable to Him for all our talents, not for only a tenth or a fifth."

" You are right, Miss Todd, I think."

" Have you ladies finished your theological discussions?" interrupted Mr. Pierce. " For my part, I look upon God as a ' Deus ex machina.' Some Force has evidently set this old world of ours going, but I don't believe He cares one jot what becomes of any of us. If He does, why is there so much sin and wickedness in the world?"

" To show us the need of a Saviour," replied Miss Todd. " But tell me, do you find much happiness in your belief, or rather unbelief?"

" More than those that are always using a microscope to examine their inner selves for germs of wickedness, or feeling their religious pulse to see if it is beating properly."

" I think, if we do what God would have us do, we shall not have much time for self-examination. But do you not think your children are happier to know that you care what becomes of them than if they were to feel that you were perfectly indifferent to their welfare ?"

" I don't think that has anything to do with the question at issue. But you are just like the rest of women, Miss Todd, always running off to a side-track. I never saw a woman that could really argue yet."

" Well, here we are back in the house orchard. Help yourselves to peaches. I wonder what kind of peaches I should have if I allowed the trees to manage themselves," said Miss Todd, with a sly smile.

" You certainly have very delicious ones. It would be hard to beat one like this," said Mr. Pierce, lifting one up that was over eight inches in circumference and very beautifully colored. " But does fruit-growing in British Columbia pay? There are so many expenses and risks connected with the industry that I am beginning to fear that I have made a mistake investing in a fruit ranch."

" Fruit-growing is like any other business—brains, patience and industry are as necessary as money. Other things being equal, a person having considerable capital will do much better than one having only a small amount. Although I have had some losses, I am well satisfied with my profits. Last year my peach orchard realized $600 an acre, and the apple orchard $400 an acre. I have four acres of

apple trees and two of peach, so that altogether my
fruit sold for $2,800; my expenses were $1,600, so
that my net profit was $1,200.  Besides what I sold,
I had all the fruit I wanted for the house.  Of course
my brother and I have the first right to the creek, as
my father recorded the water in the early days.  This
is a great advantage, as we have our own water system, thus having all the water we want, without paying water rates.  But then again, being only a woman, I have to hire quite a bit of help, and that costs
in this country; so I see no reason why you should
not do at least as well here as in Manitoba, while enjoying a much better climate.  I might say that
both my brother and I have our own markets, so that
the greater part of our profits is not swallowed up
by middlemen, as is unfortunately the case with
many of the newer growers.  What do you think of
Todd Valley, as it is sometimes called after my
father, who was the first settler?"

"I am much pleased with it; it is certainly an
ideal place.  You have not as good a view as we folks
on the benches have, but your other advantages out-
weigh that.  The ranches are in first-class condition,
with the exception of the one next to your brother's.
That is a forsaken-looking place; the fence is in a
very dilapidated condition; the weeds are as tall as
many of the trees, which don't appear to have ever
seen the pruning shears; and the buildings are in a
very poor condition, too.  I thought at first no one
was living there, but afterwards I saw some children playing around.  They looked as neglected as
their surroundings.  What is the reason that that
place is so different from the others?"

" You have surely lived long enough in the world
to make a pretty good guess at the reason.  What is
at the bottom of one-half of the misery in the world ?"

" I suppose you mean drink."

" Yes, I do, especially when the drinking habit
is combined with laziness, which is frequently the
case. Two years ago that was one of the best ranches
in this neighborhood.  The owner, wishing to give
his children better educational advantages than could
be obtained here, sold his place to the present owner,
a good-for-nothing, shiftless fellow named Ward.
The fellow came here with the queerest ideas.  Some
person had evidently been making a fool of him by
telling him that all he would have to do on a fruit
ranch would be to fold his arms and watch the trees
grow.  When he found out that hard work was
needed, he got discouraged and comforted himself
by the bottle.  I have very little sympathy for him,
and not much for his wife, who might at least try
to keep the house and children tidy; but I do feel
sorry for the poor little ones, who haven't clothes fit
to wear except those supplied by the neighbors.
What a curse to the country this liquor traffic is!  I
don't believe the evil will be removed until we women
get our rights."

" I suppose you refer to woman's franchise," said
Mr. Pierce stiffly.  "For my part, I hope women
will never get the right to vote."

" Why not?" asked Miss Todd, coolly surveying
her opponent.

" What will become of our homes and of our children when our wives and mothers are spending their
time and their energies in squabbling over politics ?"

5

"I see no reason why they should not be as well looked after as at present. Surely it does not take very long to cast a ballot. Where there is a municipality, women have a right, even in British Columbia, to vote in local matters. I know quite a few women who avail themselves of this privilege, and their homes are as well looked after as any home here where we have no municipality. At any rate, it is a violation of the fundamental principle of responsible government, 'No taxation without representation,' to deprive women who pay taxes of the right to say how those taxes should be spent; and an insult to their intelligence to class them with 'criminals and idiots.'"

"But, Miss Todd, do you really think many women would vote if they had the right to? I think I would rather leave politics to men. If we train our children aright, we shall find enough to take up our attention without bothering our heads with mighty affairs of state."

"I see it is to be a fight of one against two," laughed Miss Todd. "My dear Mrs. Pierce, granting that many women would not vote if they had the chance, should that fact deprive those who wish the right of having it? There are some men who seldom, if ever, vote. Should that fact rob all men of the franchise? I fail to see how the right to vote would disqualify a woman for training her children properly. It seems to me that the responsibility of the franchise would make mothers take a more intelligent interest in their country's welfare. Surely a woman who has thought much and deeply about the leading political questions of the day is better qualified to instruct her children in the duties of citizenship than the one who has not."

"I wouldn't give up my little woman here for all the howling suffragettes that are just now making such disgusting fools of themselves in England," said Mr. Pierce, putting his hand caressingly upon the shoulder of his wife, who treasured such caresses—too rarely given—more than many a woman does her diamonds. "There's the effect of politics on women, what do you think of it?"

"I shouldn't call that the effect of politics, but the result of lack of politics."

"How do you make that out?"

"Why, it surely isn't very politic to act in the way they are doing. They are doing more harm than good to our cause. I hope, Mr. Pierce, that you do not judge all women by them. Women have not lost their nobler feelings nor have they become less refined or less womanly in the places where they have been given their political rights. Many social reforms have been brought about in Finland, New Zealand, and other places largely by the votes and influence of women."

"Woman has a great influence over man on account of her womanly qualities; when she enters on a public career, she loses those qualities, and has less influence than if she had remained in her own sphere of life."

"You are talking theory; I am talking facts. Which is stronger? I do not see any great publicity in recording a vote, anyway."

"Perhaps not, but when women are given votes they will, I suppose, be candidates for parliamentary

honors.  Fancy a woman having to endure all the
mud-throwing that such candidates have to put up
with at the hands of their opponents!  Some of the
mud is sure to stick, then what becomes of her most
precious possession—a spotless character?"

" I do not think many women will compete for
public positions.  If some do, and they have a spotless character and should they succeed in getting into
Parliament, they might purify the political atmos-
phere, which seems to need it badly enough.  Mud-
throwing may hurt a person's reputation, it cannot
hurt his or her character; only inward impurity will
affect that."

" Outward impurity will cause inward impurity.
I tell you no woman can come in contact with the
political corruption of the present time without
moral defilement."

" Is it necessary for politics to be corrupt?"

" No, of course not, but I am talking of things as
they are.  Do you not know that many of our best
men refuse to have anything to do with politics on
account of their corrupt condition?"

" I wonder what our orchards would be like, if,
when they became infested with pests, we should say,
'They are too filthy, we shall have nothing to do with
them.'  If politics are corrupt—and I do not dispute
your statement—is it not the duty of every lover of
his country to step into the political arena and fight
the wild beasts that are preying upon the vitals of
his native land?  If there is any person I despise it
is the ' stand off, I am holier than thou ' kind.
Would you not yourself despise the man who, seeing
a poor fellow sinking in a bog, turns aside, saying,

' I might get myself dirty if I tried to help him out ' ?
I tell you, Mr. Pierce, God will hold those men who
are too cowardly or too selfish to aid in uplifting our
country from the slough of political corruption, and
who refuse to aid in making her unequalled among
the nations of the world for moral strength and
beauty as she is in natural scenery and resources,
just as responsible as those who are helping to drag
her down into the mire. I think that politics would
be purified by the introduction of women. It is
not so many years ago that a woman never attended
political meetings. What were they like then? You
can not help admitting that their character is greatly
improved by the presence of women. But I must go
and get tea ready, and cease trying to convince a person against his will."

" Like the rest of her sex, she had the last word,"
said Mr. Pierce to his wife, as Miss Todd went into
the house.

# CHAPTER IX.

## A CHARMING WIDOW.

Among the many visitors who honored Ortgeard by their presence that summer was Mrs. Yates, a very beautiful and attractive widow, whose years did not appear to be far beyond a score. At least a casual observer would not accuse her of being older than twenty-five when she was seen in all her company attire. Some people were mean enough to say that powder and paint had something to do in subtracting from her age, but those were women who were jealous of her charms. A childlike simplicity and manner added to her youthful appearance, which was still further increased by her fair complexion, dimpled cheeks, and golden hair. But her chief charm lay in her beautifully curved mouth and sparkling eyes, whose color the jealous members of her sex said was green, but which her many admirers declared to be hazel. She always dressed in perfect taste, and her calm manner and delicately inflected tone of voice showed her to have been accustomed to good society, at least such was the verdict of those who professed to be judges of such matters.

People wondered what could induce such a charming woman to stay in a small place like Ortgeard, but she declared that she was tired of city life and that she really enjoyed the peaceful quiet and beauti-

ful surroundings of this Okanagan town.   If she did
not enjoy them, it was certainly not the fault of the
hospitable people of Ortgeard, especially of the
sterner sex, for all vied in trying to gain her smiles.
As she was a good horsewoman and fond of boating,
it was not, after all, so very difficult to amuse her; at
least, so the men declared, although the women
thought otherwise.   Doubtless they were right, as
the lady herself seemed bored by the society of her
own sex, who appeared incapable of appreciating her
numerous attractions.

Among the many men honored by her favor was
Mr. Pierce, whom she pronounced to one of her few
lady friends to be the most handsome and charming
man she had ever met.

They first met at a picnic held in a beautiful grove
on the lake shore, half a mile from the Canyon
Ranch.   It was an ideal place for picnics, the water
being deep enough in the little cove formed by two
projecting bluffs to allow gasoline launches to come
close to the shore, the grove affording shelter from
the hot rays of the summer sun, and an open level
tract of land inviting athletes to display their prow-
ess in their favorite sports.   The Pierces arrived late
in the afternoon, as Mr. Pierce had not made up his
mind to go until after dinner.   At first he said that
picnics were always stupid affairs that made him feel
more tired than a day's work.   However, when he
saw the disappointed faces of Harry and May he re-
pented and said he would go " to please the kids."

On account of the heat, the sports had not yet
started and the people were enjoying themselves, or
pretending to enjoy themselves, in their own way.

"Who is that handsome man with such a distinguished air, who is just now making his appearance on the scene? Is that his wife with him? A transposed case of 'Beauty and the Beast' it seems to be. Introduce me, please."

After Mrs. Yates' wish was complied with, she at once proceeded to monopolize Mr. Pierce's time and attention; this was quite easy to do, as Mrs. Pierce was soon carried off to help get the tables ready, and the children ran off to find some of their little friends.

"Are you a resident of this place?" asked Mrs. Yates after a few minutes' conversation on ordinary topics.

"I have been since spring. I am a fruit rancher, or rather, I am trying to be one."

"I should think you will find it rather dull here in winter. I admit it is a delightful place to spend a few months in the summer, especially for those that are worn out with the season's round of gaities; but how do the natives manage to spend the winter?"

"I don't think there are any natives here. We see a few once in a while, but there are none living in the place."

"I see I must apologize. How do the residents of Ortgeard amuse themselves in the winter?"

"Having never been here in the winter, I am afraid I cannot supply you with the desired information. I fancy the most of them find plenty to do. I believe there is a Literary Society that provides entertainment for the heads, and a Quadrille Club that provides amusement for the feet of those whom you appear to pity. I wonder if that pity will go

far enough to help us pass next winter in a more
pleasant way. With such a talented and charming
leader, much might be done. There are some very
good singers among us, and also some good pianists
and violinists. I have heard that you are a good
musician; with your help we might have some very
pleasant evenings."

"I do not call myself a musician, although I sing
and play a little, more, I am afraid, for my own
amusement than to give pleasure to others. If the
ladies here were a little more sociable, I should not
mind spending a winter in Ortgeard. It would be
something new, anyway. Fancy my becoming a mis-
sionary! I wonder what my New York friends
would say if I were to do such a thing—not that I
care what they or anybody else says."

"I hope we can persuade you to stay with us
for the winter. You will not find the weather severe,
and as for the Ortgeard ladies, you can hardly blame
them for being a little bit jealous."

"Why should they be jealous?"

"Look in your mirror, and you will then be able
to answer your own question."

"I see you can flatter as well as the rest of your
sex. To change the subject, I should like a boat ride.
Do you think you could manage one?"

"I can but try," so saying he went off to secure a
boat. Having succeeded in his quest, he hurriedly
came back to Mrs. Yates, who had managed to pass
the few minutes of waiting in a pleasant flirtation
with an overgrown boy, who was trying hard to appear a man.

"I have the boat. I must see if Mary will come with us. Excuse me for a minute."

An unpleasant expression flitted for a moment over Mrs. Yates' face, but she only said, "Certainly," then resumed her conversation with her boy cavalier.

In a few minutes he returned alone.

"The women folks say that they are short of help, and cannot possibly spare my wife. We must not be gone too long, as the tables will soon be ready."

The tables were ready and the viands were being heartily enjoyed by all but the waiters, who were looking rather tired, but who probably got a good share of enjoyment out of seeing the enjoyment of the hungry and thirsty participators of the feast. The waiters at last enjoyed the reward of their labors, at least all but one did. Mrs. Pierce was so anxious at the non-arrival of her husband that she did not feel like eating anything. Nearly two hours had passed since he had gone with Mrs. Yates for a half-hour boat ride, but still there was no sign of the truants.

"Do you think anything could have happened to them?" at last she asked her neighbor at the table, a fat, pompous woman, who generally "bossed" the refreshment part of the programme at picnics and other social gatherings.

"No, of course not, what could happen? The lake is as smooth as a mill pond. No fear of that woman getting drowned. No such good luck! There now, don't look so vexed. I s'pose I've put my foot in it. I generally manage to do that. I didn't think when I was speaking that Mrs. Yates could hardly get

drowned without something happening to your husband. I don't see what the men can find so attractive
about that green-eyed widow. She reminds me more
of a rattlesnake than anything else."

"And the men are the birds, I suppose," said a
young lady who happened to hear the fat woman's
speech.

"I wasn't talking to you, Miss Fairchild. You
should be amusing your right-hand neighbor, instead
of listening to my foolish chatter."

"Oh, I have been hearing so many sensible things
lately, that I want to hear something foolish for a
change. 'Variety is the spice of life,' you know."

"Well, if you want variety, come and help clear
away these things; we're all done now, I think."

"Hadn't we better wait a little while longer for
the missing ones?" asked Miss Todd, who had been
one of the helpers.

"No, indeed, we won't. Do you suppose we are
going to miss seeing the sports for two 'lunies' that
are thinking of nothing or nobody else than themselves?"

"Come on, then, let us clear away; the baskets will
do for the truants," said Miss Todd, who was now
anxious to prevent Mrs. Pierce's being annoyed by
the pitying glances of the women.

The poor woman now began to realize that none
of them feared any accident, but that they thought
the missing ones were enjoying a pleasant flirtation.
This realization led her to resolve to resume her
wonted composure, and so well did she succeed that
nobody there, with the exception of Miss Todd, had

any idea of the painful feelings that surged in the heart of the calm-faced wife.

When the last cloth had been taken off the table, the wanderers returned hungry and quite astonished to discover that tea had been over for some time. At least Mrs. Yates declared she was astonished, but the stout woman whispered to her neighbor that she didn't see how she could be, when she had a good watch and the sun for guides.

"You really must blame Mr. Pierce, my dear ladies, for our absence; he is such an entertaining companion that I really never noticed how the time was going."

So entertaining a companion did she find him, that before the picnic was over she had resolved to sacrifice herself for the benefit of the unfortunate "natives" and spend the winter in Ortgeard.

# CHAPTER X.

## WHO GETS THE PROFITS?

THE summer was passing away, and the fruit-
ranchers were busy gathering the downy peaches, and
packing and shipping them off to some distant market. The crop was a very good one, and, although
every person looked tired, all were happy; for a
good crop means, or should mean, prosperity for the
whole community.

Although the peach trees on the Pierce ranch were
only young and had not been very well cared for,
the family were kept quite busy, busier than many
of their neighbors, as they were " green " at the
work and were unable to tell by looking whether a
peach was fit to pick or not, but had to judge by feeling, which is a very slow process. Then, also they
were much slower at packing than others, but they
all enjoyed the work, even to little May, whose task
consisted in getting rid of many of the culls.

Miss Todd had offered to buy the crop at ninety
cents a box for first-grade fruit, but Mr. Pierce, having been told that he could do better than that by
selling the peaches to a small local company, refused
her offer, much to the regret of his wife, who very
wisely said, " We know what we are going to get
when we sell to Miss Todd, and the money is sure;
but the members of this company don't seem to

know what they themselves are going to get, and do not guarantee us any fixed price."

"A dollar and ten cents a box is a good deal better than ninety cents, and Mr. Newman says that is the very least he expects for his peaches, and I'm not going to sell ours for a cent less, even to oblige Miss Todd."

Mrs. Pierce, being one of the few women who know when it is wise to be silent, said no more.

Among the many visitors who came during the season, was Mrs. Yates, who came often to learn "how to pack peaches," as she said, but Helen said "I don't believe a word she says. If she really wants to learn to pack peaches, why doesn't she go to Miss Todd, who is said to be one of the best packers in the district. She's a regular nuisance, for we don't get nearly as much done when she's here; it takes her a whole afternoon to pack one box, and she keeps father from his work and makes your work harder, for you have to wait on her so much."

"I am afraid, my dear, you are not hospitably inclined," said her mother.

"Yes, I am, mother, to those I like; but I don't like that woman one bit, and I shan't pretend to, either."

"I hope you will not be rude. You know it would annoy me very much to see one of our guests treated rudely by any of our children."

"I'll try to be as nice as I can to please you, but it will be a hard job. How I wish she would go away!"

Doubtless Mrs. Pierce wished the same thing, although she did not see fit to say so.

"My dear Mrs. Pierce, I feel so much at home here that I don't stand on ceremony, but just come whenever I feel like it," said Mrs. Yates one day, in her purring way to her hostess. "I consider I have a standing invitation to most of the places here; the people are so kind and I'm beginning to like Ortgeard so much that I'm seriously thinking of buying a fruit ranch myself, and of settling down to a quiet life."

Mrs. Pierce was not by any means a jealous woman, but she had a vague distrust of this handsome widow with her sparkling eyes, whose color was so difficult to tell. Many of Mrs. Pierce's neighbors began to whisper that she was blind if she did not see cause for jealousy, as the widow and Mr. Pierce were together on every possible occasion.

As the Pierces had no apples to sell, their busy time was practically over after the last peaches were shipped. Although there were no more peaches to pack, Mrs. Yates still continued her frequent visits, and Mr. Pierce was quite as often boating or riding with her as he was working on his place. To do him justice, he really had tried in a feeble sort of way to resist the attractions of this modern Circe, but being very fond of flattery and a pretty face, he slowly yielded to her fascinating charms, although he still loved his wife as much as it was possible for him to love anyone. Knowing this to be the fact and believing that he possessed the full confidence of his wife, he could see no harm in having a pleasant time with the American widow.

Summer passed away, followed by the beautiful autumn weather for which this famous valley is

noted; the Pierce family were now comfortably settled in their new house, but they found that a great
deal of money was going out and very little coming
in.  As yet they had not received enough from the
sale of tomatoes and cherries to pay for the boxes;
but when Mr. Pierce said anything to the secretary
of the Ortgeard Fruit Association, the answer was,
" We have not received the returns from the North-
West Company yet.  Don't worry, it'll be all right;
but I'm afraid we shan't get as much as we expected
for our fruit.  Car loads of inferior stuff came into
the North-West and glutted the market."

Mr. Pierce now began to wish he had taken his
wife's advice about selling his crop, but he would
not tell her so.

About the middle of November news came that
the North-West Company had failed, and that probably they would be able to pay only forty cents on the
dollar.  Great was the consternation in not only
Ortgeard but in many other places in  the  valley,
when the ranchers learned that they were to receive
only forty cents a box for their peaches and perhaps
not that.

After the worst was known, a meeting of fruit-
growers was held to decide what was to be done about
the next year's crop.

" I think that the best plan is to do as we did
before the local company was formed; that is, sell
to buyers at a fixed price.  We get our money then,
and without waiting six months for it either," said
one of the old-timers, a Mr. Hazard.

" That may be all right for a time or two, but it
is not wise for us to be at the mercy of buyers.  They

must have their profit, of course; then, if they sell to
a wholesale company the latter must have theirs; then
the retailer must have his; so, although the consumer
pays a good price for the fruit, the grower gets
hardly enough to pay his hired help and other expenses," said Mr. Newman, who had been one of
the strongest members of the local company.

" The proof of the pudding is in the eating. All
I know is that I never fared so badly before. This
year my expenses were a thousand dollars and my
total receipts were only $660. Two or three more
experiences like this will land me in the poorhouse,"
said another victim of the bankrupt company. "Very
likely the company failed with full pockets."

" I am sure you are wrong there," said the secretary of the local company. " Our lawyer probed the
matter to the bottom and declares he found nothing
crooked. That there was mismanagement we all
know, but still what ruined the company was not so
much mismanagement as the fact that carloads of
peaches were dumped upon the prairie markets at a
lower price than we can grow them here. Then, too,
I am credibly informed that a prominent British
Columbia buyer deliberately sold peaches in Calgary
at seventy cents a box after he had paid a dollar a
box besides the freight. First-class peaches they
were, too! Now why did he do such a foolish thing
as that? It was because he sees the formation of
co-operative companies will drive him and other
buyers out of business, so he went to work to ruin
the company that had been the best customer of the
Fruit Growers' Association in order that the pro-
ducers will become discouraged at the result of their

6

efforts at co-operation and will again become dependent on the buyers. If you are satisfied that the principle of co-operation is right, don't let the first failure or two discourage you. What has been a success in Washington and Oregon should be also one here."

" Don't forget that our American friends haven't the exorbitant freight rates to contend with that we have. With so many competing railroads they have a freight rate that enables them to sell fruit to the prairie people cheaper than we can, even after they pay the duty, which is a mere bagatelle," said another speaker.

" I think someone ought to interview the Government at Ottawa and tell them that a young and growing industry in British Columbia will be throttled by our American cousins, if a prohibitive duty is not placed at once on American fruit," was the remark of a good Conservative.

" That might help us for a year or so, but I doubt that it would be a benefit in the end," replied Mr. Newman. " I want a fair price for my fruit, but I do not want my fellow-countrymen to pay an exorbitant price for it. Even if there were a high duty placed on American fruit, as things are now, the middlemen would, I fear, get all the extra profit at the expense of the prairie consumer. No, the remedy is not a protective duty."

"What is it then ?"

" First, we must form a strong co-operative company—not a number of small local ones, none of them with sufficient capital to undertake the placing of British Columbia fruit at the door of the consum-

ers without its having to pass through the hands of
several middlemen, who swallow the profits.  By co-
operation we should be able to ship in carloads with
cold storage facilities; this would reduce the freight
charges considerably.  Another advantage of co-
operation would be that we should be in a better
position to demand cheaper freight rates from the
C. P. R.  If all the Okanagan fruit-growers could
be induced to unite, the problem would be in a fair
way of solution.  A strong company would be able
to place in the principal towns of the North-West
men whose business it would be to see that there
should not be a surplus in one place and a dearth in
another.  I think, myself, if our men could sell directly to the consumer it would be a great advantage; but if not, they could look after the proper
distribution of the fruit, and could see whether com-
plaints of fruit's arrival in a damaged condition are
groundless or not."

"That's something I should jolly well like to see,"
interrupted a gentleman who had not yet spoken.
"A friend of mine in Ontario received word from
a commission agent in Winnipeg that his shipment
of apples had arrived in such a condition that they
were almost unsaleable.  He suspected something
crooked, and at once set off for Winnipeg.  When
he arrived in that city he immediately demanded to
see the damaged apples.  After a good deal of blus-
tering on the part of both seller and agent, the latter
admitted that only five per cent. of them were
damaged, and paid a fair price for the apples.  Now,
what would have happened if my friend had not been
able to go himself or send somebody else to investi-

gate the complaint? He would have received next
to nothing for his fruit, and the agent would have
reaped the profits."

"Yes, some of these middlemen tell thundering
big lies," said an old-timer. "I remember once I
was in Vancouver when a shipment of peaches came
from the orchard of a grower whom I happened to
know. Wanting to make a present to my hostess, I
bought two boxes, but I was a good deal taken aback
when I was told the price, two dollars a box. But
they were fine peaches, and the dealer said there
were few coming in just then; so I paid the money
cheerfully, for I thought to myself, 'There'll be
money in peaches this year, anyway.' Imagine my
astonishment when my friend told me that he had
received only seventy-five cents a box for that very
shipment of peaches. When he complained he was
told that the fruit had been picked too green, conse-
quently lacked in flavor and color, and that the market was glutted. I wanted him to go to law about
it, but he refused, saying that it would cost more
than the whole thing was worth."

"May I go on now?" asked Mr. Newman, with a
smile. "You are strengthening my case considerably."

"Certainly, go on with your remedies! Your
theories are good, but the carrying them out might
be impossible," remarked Mr. Pierce.

"Another remedy is one that lies altogether with
ourselves and must be adopted, if we wish to obtain
a reputation for fair and honest dealing. There
must be uniform and honest packing of all fruit.
Let Okanagan fruit be a synonym for the best and

most reliable fruit on the market, then we need not fear our American rivals. Let us keep our culls at home, and sell only fruit that will give our valley a reputation second to none. Let no selfishness on the part of a few bar the pathway of future prosperity which, I firmly believe, lies ahead of the Okanagan fruit-grower."

After the passage of a resolution to establish a central packing house for the coming season, the meeting came to an end.

# CHAPTER XI.

## *THE RATTLER BITES.*

" THE idea of a gentleman of your attainments shutting yourself up for life in such a place as this! It would not be so bad if you were making money, but, according to your own account, you are losing instead of winning. I have influence across the line, and if you will come to Chicago, you can enter a business in which you will make more money in one year than you will the rest of your life here." Such were the words that greeted the ears of Mr. Pierce as he and Mrs. Yates were enjoying the first boat ride of the year.

Never had there been such a merry winter as the past, was the unanimous verdict of the Ortgeard people, and the majority acknowledged that they owed their pleasure to the charming widow and her first assistant, Mr. Pierce. Whether the winter had passed as pleasantly to Mrs. Pierce as to her husband might be doubted, as she had been unable to attend any more than one or two of the meetings of the Society. " Duty before pleasure," was her motto, whereas the reverse was that of her husband. Little May had been ill the greater part of the winter, and Mrs. Pierce felt that she could not leave her in the long evenings to the care of Helen, who had her school duties to attend to, and, moreover, was not a

very acceptable nurse to the fevered little sufferer,
whose petulance could be soothed only by " mamma."

Why shouldn't he accept the widow's offer? Fruit-
farming did not give him any scope for his varied
talents. But his family, what was he to do with
them? Living in a city was expensive; that he had
found out to his cost in his early married life, when
the family consisted of only himself and his wife.
Then where was the money to come from?

Instead of consulting his wife, he explained the
difficulties of his position to his new friend. "I am
delighted with your confidence, my dear Mr. Pierce.
Now, I feel that you regard me as a friend; but
why should it be Mr. and Mrs. now between us? My
name is Julia, I know yours is Guy, so Guy and
Julia let it be," she said in one of her sweetest tones.
" Of course it would not do for you to move your
family until you got comfortably settled in your new
home. As for the money, could you not raise enough
on your place?"

Raise money on the place? He had not thought
of that, but why should he not do so? True it was,
according to justice, his wife's; but he had bought
it in his own name, though with her money, so, according to law, it was his—his to mortgage, to sell
or do with it what he liked without either the knowledge or consent of her whom he had solemnly
promised to love and cherish while life lasted. Well,
if he could do better by going to the States, was it not
his duty to do so? Mary's strength had been a great
deal tried by May's illness, so she must not be told
anything that would cause her to fret. How noble
it was of him to put upon his own shoulders the bur-

den of worry that the raising of the money would
cause! In a year, or perhaps less, if he were successful, which of course he would be, he would be able
to lift the mortgage and send for his family. Then
his wife would thank him for his loving care of her
and the children.

Long as it takes to write these thoughts down on
paper, they were only a few moments passing
through the mind of Mr. Pierce, who, before he left
his enchantress, had fully decided to adopt her advice.

Accordingly, the patient wife was much astonished and grieved to hear her husband say that he
had a good business offer in Chicago, and that he
intended to accept it.

"Surely we can make our living in Canada, without going across the line. I don't think I shall like
living there. I did so hope that this was to be our
last move. I admit we were unfortunate last season,
but things will be better arranged this one. Although
at first I did not want to come here, I like the place
and the people very much now. The climate is so
pleasant, the scenery so lovely, the people so friendly,
and our place is looking so well now, that I would
rather live on two meals a day than live in Chicago,
surrounded by every conceivable luxury."

"Nonsense! I should be a fool to refuse such a
chance. I am sorry you don't like leaving here, but
you don't like moving anyway, and yet you always
fall on your feet in the new place after all. When
you've been in Chicago a few months, you won't
want to come back here for the best ranch in the
place."

" If you have fully made up your mind to go, I shall try my best to become reconciled to the idea. My home is where you and the children are, and I hope to find happiness in seeking to make that home a pleasant place, no matter where it may be."

" I believe you're the best wife a man ever had," said he, folding her in his arms. At that moment he felt she was worth a dozen Mrs. Yates. But he had been bitten by the snake, though he knew it not, and he did not realize that in accepting the proposal of the temptress, he was putting himself in her power.

When he told Mrs. Yates that his wife had consented to his plan, and that he hoped soon to have a comfortable home for her and the children in Chicago, a strange look came into those eyes—a look that sent a deadly chill through his body, but that look lasted only a moment, then it changed into one of gentleness and womanly tenderness.

Spoken—" There can be no doubt that you will be able to do better for your charming family there than here."

Thought—" He is not weaned from that woman yet. I can't see what he finds so charming about her. Never mind, there are not many men whom I cannot turn round my little finger; and once I get him away from here, I'll not find much trouble managing Mr. Pierce."

The next week Ortgeard lost its most charming visitor, and the week after Mrs. Pierce tearfully bade farewell to her husband.

# CHAPTER XII.

## THE POISON WORKS.

"You needn't think so much of yourself, Harry Pierce. Your father had to mortgage his place to get enough money to go away with."

"What a liar you are, Dick Newman! Our place isn't mortgaged one bit. You are talking through your hat. When you get mad you never know what you say."

"I know what I'm saying now, you bet! I ought to know when my father holds the mortgage. If you don't believe me, ask him."

"I'll do it, too, just as soon as I get home. Then you'll catch it from your father for telling lies!"

"Not much! Ask him as soon as you like;" so saying Dick Newman, with a shrug of contempt for his dearest chum of ten minutes ago, but now, owing to some childish quarrel, his bitterest enemy, he ran home.

He had not been home ten minutes before a loud knock at the hall-door proclaimed a visitor. The visitor was Harry, who with flushed face asked to see Mr. Newman. This gentleman at once went to the door, and asked the little visitor to come into the sitting-room.

"No, thank you; I can't stay. Dick said you had a mortgage on our place. It isn't true, is it?"

"He said so, did he, the young scamp! What business is it of his, I'd like to know, to be talking nonsense?"

"Then it isn't true, after all. I'm so glad," said Harry, looking so delighted that Mr. Newman felt like an executioner when he said:

"I'm not saying it is not true, but whether true or not, it is certainly not proper for you boys to be talking about your parents' affairs."

"But I want to know the truth. Please, Mr. Newman, do tell me," said the boy with quivering lips.

Inwardly vowing revenge on his meddlesome son, he said: "Yes, it is true, but don't worry about it. The sum borrowed is not very large, and I daresay your father will soon be able to pay it off. To have a mortgage on one's place is no disgrace. Lots of people have their places mortgaged these hard times. Now don't, my boy, don't." Then Mr. Newman placed his hand kindly on the shoulder of the boy, who was now crying bitterly.

"I—I—can't—help it," said Harry through his sobs. "I hate mortgages and I know mother hates them, too, for I've heard her say she would sooner live on one meal a day than have her place mortgaged. But I must not be a baby. I think I'll leave school and stay home to work, so we can get this hateful thing paid off."

"Your father will see to that, let us hope; but you are a fine boy and will be a great help to your mother some day," were Mr. Newman's parting words.

"Humph!" he soliloquized, after his little visitor had departed; "that lad is more of a man than his father. I wonder now if Pierce was mean enough to borrow money on his place without saying a word to his wife about it. I suppose that's law in this blessed province, but it ain't justice, and it couldn't be done in good old Ontario. There the wife, who, in the majority of cases, has had her share in making the place, has something to say about such things. Bless my life! I'm sorry I had anything to do with it. But I don't know after all. That fellow was bound to get money somehow, and if things come to the worst, Mrs. Pierce will not find me a hard man to deal with."

"Mother, I want to leave school," said Harry shortly after he had gone home.

"Leave school! What nonsense! I thought you like going to school better than staying at home?"

"So I do, mother, but now father is away I am needed at home."

"Your place is at school and will be for a few more years. What we can't do ourselves we must hire help to do. I would not think of such a foolish thing as keeping you home from school."

"But, mother, if we have to hire help, how shall we get the mortgage paid off?"

"Mortgage! What are you talking about, darling?"

"Oh, mother, don't you know? Daddy borrowed money from Mr. Newman to go away, and so he holds a mortgage on his place," said Harry, regardless in his distress of the confusion of pronouns. "It's true; he told me so to-night."

"Who told you?"

"Mr. Newman! But don't look that way, dear mother! Oh, I wish I hadn't told you!"

With a great effort Mrs. Pierce regained her usual calm self-possessed manner, but like the bird with the broken pinion, she "could never soar so high again." That he, whom she had so loved and trusted, should have mortgaged the place that had been bought with her own money, without saying a word to her, was indeed a bitter blow to her faith in him.

After she had gone to her own room for the night she sat for hours in her low bedroom rocker thinking about what Harry had told her. At first she tried to make herself think that it could not be true, but then again she knew that Mr. Newman would not have said so if it had not been the fact. Then, too, had she not herself wondered where her husband obtained the money necessary for his new venture? She had wondered, but she had not thought of asking him, as that would have been displaying a lack of confidence in him. For a few bitter moments it seemed to her that her love as well as her faith had received a blow from which it would never recover. But that love was like a sweet-scented geranium leaf, crushed it might be, but its fragrance was all the sweeter. "O God," she prayed, "let me not lose my faith and love. Forgive my bitter thoughts and help me to be a good wife to my husband. Keep him safe and bring us together again."

## CHAPTER XIII.

### PHILIP HASTINGS TO THE RESCUE.

"MY DEAR COUSIN:

"In your last letter you wondered why you had not heard from Mrs. Pierce for such a long time. It isn't good news I have to tell you, I fear. I suppose the reason she hasn't written lately is that she doesn't feel like it.

"You know that I told you in a former letter that Mr. Pierce had gone to seek his fortune in the States. Seek his fortune, the scamp! The most of the people here say that it is to seek the company of the fair widow with whom he was so friendly last winter, and I'm afraid they are not far from the truth.

"Like a meddlesome woman as I am, when you told me that it was Mrs. Pierce's own money that bought the fruit-ranch, I made it a point to call on her and to give her a hint that she'd better have the place in her own name if she wanted to save herself and children from the injustice of British Columbia law. But do you suppose she'd listen to me? Not a bit! She got quite angry, at least as angry as such a sweet-tempered woman could get. How Guy Pierce could leave such an angel of a woman as his wife to be with that bold-faced hussy, I can't con-

94

ceive. I suppose he thinks the widow an angel, too. Well, so she is, but one of another kind.

"Pierce hasn't written to his wife for a long time, unless he wrote since I saw her last night. I asked her then if she had heard from him lately, and she admitted she hadn't, but excused his neglect by saying he was very busy. Yes, I suppose he is busy gallivanting around with that snake. I call her a snake, for she reminds me of one every time I think of her. I don't whisper any of my suspicions to Mrs. Pierce. I'd as lief knock her on the head as do it; but other people have not been so careful; I'm sure she has heard some of the talk, for she looks real bad, although she tries to go around with a brave face for the children's sake.

"But, for the land's sake, how I do wander from my subject! What I started to tell you was that Pierce mortgaged the place for $1,500 to get money for his new venture in the States. Just think of it, Cousin Anne, putting a heavy load of debt on the place bought with his wife's money without saying, 'By your leave' to her. Who's going to pay the interest? Who's going to work the place? Wonder if he expects that delicate woman to do a man's work on the place, look after her house and children and pay the interest on that dreadful mortgage! To tell the truth, I don't believe he thinks about those things at all. If he's having a good time he won't worry about other people; at least that's my opinion about Mr. Guy Pierce."

Here Mrs. Hicks stopped reading Miss Todd's letter, and, turning to Mr. Hastings for sympathy, said:

"Do you know what that Guy Pierce has gone and done now? He's mortgaged his wife's place in Ortgeard, and gone to the States with another woman."

"What! He couldn't mortgage his wife's place without her consent."

"I s'pose he called it his, but it was bought with her money, anyway. She's left in a pretty bad way, I'm afraid. Here's my cousin's letter. There ain't no secrets in it. Read for yourself."

Mr. Hastings dropped the newspaper he had been reading, and with trembling fingers took the letter in his hand. His face grew white as he read the contents of the letter referring to the Pierces, and in his excitement he crushed the letter in his hand, forgetting it was not his own. Then, realizing what he was doing, he smoothed it out, and with a few words of apology handed the letter to Mrs. Hicks, then left the room.

Two days later he said to his housekeeper:

"I have sold my property here and am going to Ortgeard to see if I can't find some fruit land to buy. My nephew is in British Columbia now and he likes it very well. I can't get him to come back to Manitoba, so I shall try to get him to live with me there. I hope you won't object to the change of abode. You'll be near your cousin, Miss Todd, and we're both getting too old to stand these cold winters."

"You getting too old! Not a bit of it, but I'd like first-rate to be where I could see Cousin Hannah once in a while. She's odd in her ways, but she's

the real thing, after all. Then I should like to be
near dear Mrs. Pierce again. If it's all true what
this letter says, and Hannah doesn't say things that
aren't true—at least what she doesn't believe to be
true—she'll need all her friends."

"I'm glad that you are willing to go with me. I
should feel lost without you to give me a scolding
once in a while."

"When are we to go?"

"I should like to start Tuesday at the latest. I'm
taking a car, so there will be quite a bit of packing
to do. But the men and I will all help."

"That's pretty short notice, but I think I can get
ready by then."

"My! who'd ever have thought that I'd be in
Ortgeard so soon after the Pierces' going! Strange
things happen," said Mrs. Hicks to herself after
Mr. Hastings had left the room. Then with a sly
smile, "Philip Hastings had no more idea of selling
his place and going off to British Columbia before he
read that letter than he had of going to the moon.
I'm as sure of that as I am that my name is Anne
Hicks. But what he can do when he does get there for
that poor, dear woman is more than I can tell. Not
but what I'm pleased that he is going, for I'm sure
he'll help her if she'll let him. I'm afraid she'll be
too proud to let him help her, at least in the way of
money. What fools women are anyway, to give all
their property to their husbands! If all men were
like Philip Hastings or my good man, who would
have died rather than wrong any woman, it wouldn't
matter so much, but they ain't, more's the pity."

7

Late in October, to the surprise of their friends, Mr. Hastings and his housekeeper arrived in Ortgeard.

Miss Todd gave a warm invitation to the newcomers to stay with her until Mr. Hastings would have time to look around, but, although he spent one pleasant afternoon at her place, he refused to accept it for himself, but was pleased to do so for his housekeeper.

On the evening of his arrival, when Mrs. Pierce went to open the door in response to a hasty rap, she was confused and pleased to see her old friend. Pleased because she had always regarded him as a friend who would be true in adversity, but confused because she did not wish him to know the straits in which she was placed.

But although her feelings were mixed, those of the children were pure, for in their joy there was no alloy. They welcomed him heartily, and the first hour of his visit to the deserted family was spent in answering the numerous questions of the eager children. When they had retired to rest, Mr. Hastings at once introduced his business.

"You know, Mrs. Pierce, that your father and I were warm friends; now for the sake of that friendship will you not look upon me as you would have looked upon him were he still alive, and rely upon me for any assistance that I can render you."

"You are very kind, but I am expecting to hear from my husband every mail. If he should be ill, I might need to borrow money to go to him, but otherwise we can get along without any financial help. We had a fair crop this year, and when the money

comes for our fruit, will be quite comfortable."
This was said by Mrs. Pierce a little stiffly, as if she
felt that Hastings doubted her husband's honor, and,
therefore, wished him to realize that she would regard it as an insult did he even dare to hint at any
lack of respect and love on the part of that husband.

"Will you promise that, if you should need help,
you will ask me for it instead of applying to a
stranger? For the sake of your children you have
no right in your foolish pride to reject my offer of
help. Of course you are at liberty to consider any
money given, in case you should need it, in the light
of a loan to be repaid upon your husband's return."

"Thank you ever so much for your offer. Although I hope I shall not need to do so, if unfortunately I should require aid, it will be you and not a
stranger I shall ask."

"I am glad that you put that much confidence in
me. Believe me when I say it shall not be abused.
I shall bring Mrs. Hicks to see you to-morrow, if that
will be convenient for you."

After Mr. Hastings' departure Mrs. Pierce could
not help feeling that his presence in the place was a
source of comfort to her. Then, too, how pleasant it
would be to have dear old Mrs. Hicks again to talk
to, or rather to listen to, as the part of a listener was
generally the one played by any one in the presence
of the good lady!

Not a week passed before Mr. Hastings was the
proprietor of one of the best fruit-ranches in the
place, only half a mile from Ferncliff, Mr. Pierce's
place. As there was a comfortable house on the

ranch, he and Mrs. Hicks were soon settled in their new home.

Naturally there was a good deal of intercourse between the two houses, but there was certainly nothing to warrant the cruel slanders that were being circulated by the gossips of Ortgeard. Truly the tongue is a powerful weapon for evil when used by a woman who, in her desire to have something to talk about, does not scruple to tear an innocent woman's reputation to pieces. Of such women Ortgeard had its share, and a few careless words uttered by one of this class to another of kindred nature were enough to blacken the reputation of a saint.

"I guess Mr. Pierce had good reason to leave home! That Philip Hastings is an old flame of his wife's, from what I hear. It looks mighty queer— to say the least—to see him come here and buy a place for a good deal more than it is worth, just as soon as he finds out that Pierce is out of the road. Why, Mrs. Dixon says there's hardly a day that he isn't over there, or some of them over at his place! Sech goin's on are shameful, I say. I never did like that woman, anyway; she held her head too high for me, jest as if I wasn't a good deal better than her any day. I does my duty by my husband anyway, that I does," and the virtuous Mrs. Wood looked around her as if she challenged any of her hearers to deny the truth of her statement.

"Yes, your husband certainly looks as if you did your duty so far as he is concerned, for he is the meekest man I ever saw. I can't say that I have a fancy for hen-pecked husbands, myself, though. But I should like to know whether you or Mrs. Dixon are doing your duty to your neighbor by uttering such vile slanders as this that I came just in time to hear. It's a pity an old neighbor can't be friendly to a woman whose father was one of his best friends, when he meets her in a strange place, without meddlesome gossips dishing up a mess of scandal of which no really good woman or man wishes to partake," said Miss Todd, who had come to this meeting of " The Ladies' Aid " to work, not to gossip.

" I'd like to know what call you have to make fun of my husband. It's easy to see that you needn't fear any scandal about yourself, for no one would suspect any man with eyes in his head taking a fancy to you," said Mrs. Wood, scornfully surveying the last speaker.

" ' Handsome is that handsome does,' I say," remarked a quiet woman, who, wishing to prevent an unpleasant quarrel, now let her voice be heard, " so let us leave our neighbors alone and go on with our sewing."

The efforts of the little peacemaker were successfut, but the words had done more harm than any person in the room dreamed. One of the ladies present was one of the few of the gentle sex who thought it worth while to correspond with Mrs. Yates. She, in the dearth of interesting news that prevails in a small place, retailed all she had heard, and, as such things do not lose anything in the telling, more than all, to her worthy friend. As to what use the widow made of her information, must be left to another chapter to disclose.

# CHAPTER XIV.

## THE BLOW FALLS.

MRS. PIERCE had been right in fearing that her husband was ill, but wrong in supposing that this illness was the sole reason of his neglecting to write to her. As the handsome widow boarded in the same house, she took upon herself the duties of a nurse, and so agreeable a companion did she prove that the patient was in danger of becoming like some hospital inmates who are so comfortable that they sham illness to prevent their being sent adrift. Not that our hero was capable of descending to such a contemptible trick as this, but he reasoned to himself, "Why should I distress Mary by telling her I am ill? She'll worry about it and perhaps want to come here to nurse me and there isn't the least need of that, I'm sure." So it was not until he was convalescent that he took the trouble to write, but this letter never reached its destination. Why it did not, Mrs. Yates could, if she had chosen to do so, have told. Neither did this estimable woman inform the anxious wife of her husband's illness or of his present address.

His illness and previous expenses had nearly drained the supply of money he had obtained from the mortgage, so that there was little left to invest in the business that Mrs. Yates had recommended to him. His allowance was not yet due, and altogether

the outlook was a dreary one, or would have been
had he not had the inestimable privilege of Mrs.
Yates's tender sympathy.

It was on one of the few occasions of his thoughts
going homewards and to his prospects of securing a
home for his family in the busy city of Chicago,
that Mrs. Yates entered the small sitting-room where
he was sitting in the character of a convalescent in
a very comfortable Morris chair. She had a letter
in her hand, and her face betrayed only keen sorrow
and sympathy to the unsuspecting victim, whose eyes
caught sight of the Canadian stamp.

"Have you a letter from Ortgeard?" he asked
eagerly.

"Yes," was the answer, given slowly, as if in re-
luctance.

"What's wrong? I know there's something wrong
by your face and by the way you speak. My wife
and children—are any of them sick? Speak, please,
and don't keep me in suspense."

"Your wife and children are well, or, at least,
were when this letter was written."

"Then what's the matter? For Heaven's sake,
tell me."

"Here is the letter; it will be better for you to read
it for yourself. Remember, when you do so, that
you have one woman's sympathy and love." So saying she placed the letter in his trembling hands and
quietly left the room.

Varied were Mr. Pierce's emotions as he read
the cruel slander in the letter. A man may allow his
own affections to stray to some unlawful object, but
that does not tend to make him any more tolerant

of infidelity on the part of his wife, whose duty is
to love and cherish till death, whereas in his own
opinion *his* duty is to love and cherish until he sees
a fairer face. Knowing as he did that Mr. Hastings
had been an unsuccessful rival of his in the past,
and having had no answer from his letter written
nearly a month before, and judging that his wife was
indignant at his conduct, it is perhaps little wonder
that he believed the contents of the letter. Hatred
of his rival in the affections of his wife, anger at the
thought of that wife's perfidious conduct, love for his
children whom he might never see again, unholy joy
that he was now free to love her who had been so
kind to him and had confessed to him her love—all
these emotions struggled for pre-eminence in the
heart of this unhappy yet rejoicing husband.

"I should like to have hold of that fellow for just
half an hour. Wouldn't I lower his pride? I did
think, though, that he had too much honor to steal
another man's wife. Things do look black against
him, though, for why should he sell his property in
Manitoba and buy in Ortgeard just as soon as I leave
the scene? I did think that Mary loved me well
enough to forgive my mortgaging the place without
consulting her. Confound that fellow! I'd like to
give him a hiding."

While Mr. Pierce was studying some scheme of
revenge on his erring wife and her lover, Mrs. Yates
re-entered the room.

The result of the deliberations that ensued was
seen in two letters that reached the innocent but unfortunate woman a few months after the receipt of
the deadly missive. The first letter was from Mr.

Pierce, informing his wife that he had sold the Ort-geard property as she had found somebody else to look after her, and that he was suing for a divorce, "not on the ground that I might allege, but for in-compatibility; this I do for the sake of the children, who are still dear to me." The second letter was from a Chicago lawyer, informing her that the divorce suit was filed against her and asking her to take steps to defend herself, if she cared to do so.

It is said that the nerves of the human body are capable of feeling pain only to a certain extent; that after a certain degree of suffering is reached, they be-come numb. This is true in the case of mental suf-fering, also. The blow falls, the anguish is terribly keen at first, in fact, unbearable, then exhausted nature allows a sort of mental paralysis to take place. To the victim all sense of feeling seems lost, never to be regained, as if it matters not what else befalls. But such a condition as this is only a " death in life," and is often the precursor of death itself.

Conscious of her own integrity of purpose, Mrs. Pierce could not understand why her husband should write such a cruel letter. She had never regarded Philip Hastings in any other light than that of a trustworthy friend, nor had she ever had any reason to think that his feelings were any warmer than her own. It was not so much the loss of the place, for she did not realize at the time what that meant, but it was the accusation of infidelity that wounded her so deeply. The immediate effect of the blow was so numbing that it seemed to her as if she were an on-looker pitying some miserable woman who had been

vilely insulted by her own husband.   Then this
strange sense of unreality passed away to be followed
by indignation, jealousy and anger.

" That Yankee widow has had a hand in this, I am
sure.  She hasn't those snaky eyes for nothing.  But
there are plenty of young men for her to charm, without trying to fascinate married men.  How could
Guy believe such a vile slander as this he mentions?
Somebody has been making free of my name.  How
could any woman be so cruel?  I have never harmed
anyone in the place.  Why couldn't gossips leave
me and my affairs alone?  But if Guy hadn't been
thinking more of that woman than he had any right
to, he wouldn't have been so ready to believe the
cruel slander.  I trusted him in spite of suspicious
appearances, why couldn't he trust me?  May God
forgive him!  I don't feel as if I ever could.  Let
him do as he likes; I shall not lower myself by trying in any way to defend my conduct, for there is
nothing that needs defence.  But what the children
and I are going to do now, I don't know and somehow
I don't seem to care.  Nothing matters much now."

# CHAPTER XV.

## TRUE FRIENDS.

SHORTLY after the receipt of the two letters from Chicago, Mrs. Pierce was formally informed that she was a divorced woman. She had now lost both property and husband; the house in which she lived, and which her money had built, and the labor which she and the children had put on the place, were to enrich a stranger; her good name, which she valued more than any material possession, was made a plaything for cruel gossips to tarnish with slanderous tongues. Nothing seemed left to her except her children and her faith in God. Sometimes in her darker moments doubts of a superintending Providence over the affairs of men came into her mind.

Though never a very robust woman she had always been healthy and energetic, but now she had received such a blow that her health began rapidly to fail. Dreading to meet the inquisitive glances of people who knew her story, she kept at home and dwelt a good deal more than was good for her on her trouble. Occasionally she went to church, but after the first two or three times she went no more. The cold looks that were cast on her by many of the members of her own church, the " stand to one side, I am holier than thou " manner of these good people, chilled her sensitive nature so that she resolved to stay at home in the future. The state of her health soon began to be sufficient excuse for her absence.

We imprison those who rob a person of his purse, but no punishment is meted out to those who rob him of that which is far more valuable, his good name. Indeed, the reputation thieves themselves were the first to perform the part of the Levite, and with a contemptuous shrug of the shoulder "pass by on the other side."

But the reader must not suppose that all the good people of Ortgeard were uncharitable. Among the few friends that remained to the unfortunate victim of slander, man's perfidy, woman's unscrupulousness, and British Columbia Law were Miss Todd and Mr. Hastings, the innocent cause of the worst of the trouble.

The latter, as soon as he heard of the loss of property and husband (perhaps in his opinion the first loss was greater than the second), called to see if he could render any assistance. Before doing so, however, having obtained the name of the purchaser of the Pierce property, he bought the place at a much higher figure than that for which it had been sold. Why did he do this? His reasons for doing so will be discovered later.

"You promised, Mrs. Pierce, to let me know if you were in need of any financial assistance, but you have not done so. I don't think you have treated me as a friend. What do you intend doing? Will you not tell me?"

Nobody who heard the cold business-like tone of the speaker would have suspected the volcano below the surface.

" I have been thinking of writing to the purchaser, asking him to allow us to remain on the place to work it for him. I heard that he bought it only as a speculation, and that he does not intend to live on it. The proceeds of this year's crop will supply our wants during the winter."

" Can a woman in your state of health and three children work this place ?"

" We can but try," was the brave answer.

" This trouble is killing you," sternly said her visitor.

" Perhaps. If it were not for the children, I should not care how soon the end comes," was the bitter remark.

" Will you let me help you ?"

" How ?"

" I have bought the farm from the late purchaser. Will you take it from me as a gift ? It is only giving you what is really yours. I am rich and therefore shall never miss what I have paid for it; and the happiness that I should enjoy in seeing you again the possessor of your own will amply repay me for what I have done."

" No! no! I could not think of taking such a gift from you. You are very generous, but it would never, never do."

" Why not ?"

For answer, Mrs. Pierce quietly went to her writing desk, and, taking from it the letter from her husband which had hurt her far more than the loss of her property, handed it to her friend with the words, "Read this."

"The scoundrel! How dare he write such a vile letter! No woman could have been a more faithful wife than you have been. Too faithful, I think, for you should have thought of your children's interests as well as your husband's. It is easy to find an excuse when one wants to commit a wrong against an innocent person. Somebody has slandered both of us, and Guy Pierce was only too glad to make use of the cruel slander. So far as I am concerned, I don't care much what people say, but if I hear anyone saying a word against you, I shall do my best to make him eat his words. But I do not think that because the gossips of this place have been busy telling lies about us that you should reject my offer."

"No, I cannot accept your gift. Please do not ask me."

"Would you not accept it from your husband?" asked Hastings, tremblingly.

"I have no husband. I am that most miserable and despised being, a divorced woman."

"You are a free woman, free now to marry one whom honor forbade to tell his love, one who has loved you in silence since your gentle hands bound up his wound, one who feels strong enough to face the world in your behalf, one who feels that the rest of his life will be well spent if he may be allowed to devote that portion of his life to your service. Think no more of him who has forsaken wife and children to gratify his own selfish passions. Can you not trust me with the happiness of yourself and that of your children?"

Mrs. Pierce could hardly realize that the man to whose passionate outburst she was listening was indeed the calm, self-restrained Philip Hastings. Twice during this impassioned speech she had in vain tried to interrupt him. At last she succeeded in getting him to listen to her.

"Stop, for God's sake, stop! Was not my burden of sorrow heavy enough before? I never dreamt of this. I see that my husband—I can't stop calling him that—had some reason to be jealous. Did he know your feeling for me?"

"Yes, he was kind enough to call one night before you were married to warn me that I was trespassing. God knows I wish that we had met before you had ever seen his handsome face. I might, then, have won you for my own, and you would have been saved all this misery. But why do you look so despairing? Have you no encouragement to offer me?"

"None," was the firm reply.

"Why, do you not trust me?"

"Yes, I believe that you would make a good husband, but I should not make you a good wife."

"Allow me to be the best judge of that," was the eager response.

"It is useless talking. Even if I loved you I could not feel that I was doing right to marry you. I promised at God's altar to love, honor, and obey Guy until death parted us. We are parted, not by death, but by United States law. In God's sight, I feel that I am still a wife. And, strange as it may appear to you, I still love Guy Pierce, the father of my children. I have always looked upon you as a friend, never, for even a moment, as a lover."

"Pierce little knows what a noble wife he has discarded for a woman who—according to report—is not worthy to breathe the same air. I see I have given you only fresh pain by allowing my feelings to get the better of me. I hope I have not, by confessing my love, lost your friendship."

" No, I shall be pleased to regard you as a true, unselfish friend, who forgot himself once, but only once." After a few moments' hesitation, Mrs. Pierce continued, " I am going to show you that I consider you as worthy of trust and confidence by asking a great favor from you."

" What is it ?" was the eager question.

" I feel that my days are numbered. Now, you doubtless have guessed the favor for which I am going to ask you. It is that I may leave my worse than orphaned children in your care."

" Indeed you may, but why talk of dying? You may survive me, you are much younger than I am."

" Younger in years, but older in suffering. I am sure that I am not mistaken, and your promise has relieved me from a load of care."

That night Mrs. Pierce enjoyed a better rest than any she had had before the blow came.

But Mr. Hastings was not the only true friend she found in her trouble. Many who had at first looked at her askance now discovered their mistake; and, believing her to be a noble but badly treated wife, vied in showing her their friendship. Pleased and comforted as she was to see this change of front, she could not regard those who had doubted her innocence with the same feeling as that which she felt towards Miss Todd, whose confidence and loyalty had never faltered for a moment. Her friendship did not consist in words only, but in deeds. It was largely due to Miss Todd's exertions in her behalf that the cloud of suspicion had rolled away in spite of the hateful innuendoes of the very few women who took more delight in thinking evil than in thinking good.

One spring day Miss Todd made one of her many friendly visits to Ferncliff. She, as well as Mr. Hastings, had an offer to make, but she hardly knew how to broach the subject. At last, after thinking seriously for some time, she said:

" I wish I lived nearer you so that I could see you oftener. I don't like your looks one bit. You really need some busybody like myself to look after you and to make you go out more. Now, please don't take offence at a proposition I have to make. It is that you and I go into partnership. My house is too large for me and the children as it is, and with a small addition will make a very comfortable dwelling for two families. You can go halves in paying for hired labor, and I am willing to give you one-third of the proceeds. Think how pleasant it will be for all of us to be together!"

Tears fell from her eyes as Mrs. Pierce answered, " Your nature is too transparent for deception, my dear friend. Do you think I do not see that I should reap nearly all the benefit of the transaction, did I consent to it?"

" Now, Mrs. Pierce, I assure you that it is pure selfishness on my part that leads me to make the offer. Your children will be invaluable as helpers on the place, and our two heads together will certainly be better than mine alone."

8

"I certainly would have availed myself of your very kind offer, had I not only yesterday bought this place from Mr. Hastings on terms so easy that I think we shall be able to manage, even should there be a failure of crops once in a while. I am fortunate in my children; Helen is developing into quite a sensible woman, and Harry is my right-hand helper outside. He is quite delighted with the thought that by a reasonable amount of industry, he may, by the time he is of age, be able to pay for the place."

Miss Todd's eyes brightened as she said, "I am so glad to hear this good news. What a splendid fellow that Philip Hastings is! I wonder that he never married; he doesn't appear to be a woman-hater, and I think he would make an ideal husband. Mrs. Hicks says no man could be more unselfish and attentive to a woman's comfort than he is. She says she believes that he has loved somebody who was fool enough not to love him."

With a heightened color Mrs. Pierce remarked, "Unfortunately, love is not a feeling that can be forced. It is as free and unrestrained as the air we breathe."

"I believe that Mrs. Hicks was right when she said that Mrs. Pierce was the cause of that noble man's remaining single. What simpletons some women are! If a man is good-looking and has a smooth tongue, no matter how black his heart may be, he will have half a dozen girls falling in love with him at a time," thought Miss Todd as she drove home.

# CHAPTER XVI.

## THE FIVE LEVELS.

" IF ever a person in this world reaches the highest level of life, I believe you have reached it now," said Miss Todd sorrowfully one July afternoon, as she was sitting by the lounge on which her friend was lying.

" Do not flatter me. There is a good deal of the old Adam in me yet. But what do you mean by the highest level of life?" asked Mrs. Pierce.

" I read an article the other day which interested me very much. The German professor, Fichte, spoke of five levels of life, and the writer of this article described them. Would you care to hear about them?"

" Certainly, nothing would please me better."

" I wish I could tell you the writer's own words, but I'll do the best I can. The lowest level is the Drifting Life—a life which I fear is very common. Those who, having no minds of their own, allow themselves to be influenced by others to do very foolish things—things even hurtful to their best interests; who cry out, 'What will the world say?' when asked to do something for the benefit of their fellow-men; who at the command of fashion do not hesitate to perform acts of the greatest cruelty, are living on the lowest plane or level of life. Life on this low level can not really be called life, it is only existence. The world has never been made better by people who are like a woman who, when asked why she used tight-bearing reins on her carriage horses when they could pull so much better without them, said, 'Other folks use them and have used them for years and there are still plenty of horses. That's reason enough for me.' The world can do without the drifters. They are not worthy of hatred, only of contempt.

"The second level is the Self-Centered one. It may not at first thought appear any higher than that of the drifter, but surely the man who has strength of purpose enough to refuse to be led by the nose, and pursues his own aims, regardless of that bugbear 'They say,' is as much higher in the scale of humanity than the former, as a wolf is higher than a jelly fish. Even though the aims of such a person are selfish, he can hardly benefit himself without benefiting somebody else. The man who is industrious, thinks for himself and acts accordingly, increases the value of his neighbor's property by increasing that of his own. If he be a married man, his family's interests are his also, and although 'Number One' is his motto, he is a more valuable asset in the community than the drifter."

"He may be a very dangerous one, too," remarked Mrs. Pierce.

"True, a wolf is more dangerous than a jelly fish, but nobody can deny that it is on a higher scale of life than the latter.

"The third level is the Self-Controlled Life. He who subdues his baser impulses and desires in order that he may attain some future good is living such a life. The crucifixion of the lower self, although it may be done only to benefit himself or his family, must ennoble the character.

" The fourth level is the Unselfish Life or the Altruistic. The Good Samaritan, John Howard, Wilberforce, Livingstone and Sir John Eliot lived this life. The world is richer for such lives. Take out of it all persons who take an interest in their fellow-men, who are willing to suffer toil, hardships, scorn, persecutions, even death itself in order that some poor brother may be lifted to a higher level, and you make this world of ours a hell, awful enough to suit the most severe theologian of the Middle Ages.

" Now I come to the highest level. My writer called it the God-Controlled Life. A self-controlled life is much higher and nobler than a ' They say ' controlled one, but that life which is controlled by God is the highest of all. It is the unselfish life submitted to the supreme control of Him who makes no mistakes. He who is not doing his very best to make his own corner of the world happier and better, whose heart is not filled with love for his fellows and for his God, is not living this life. The path that leads to this highest level is often one of thorns; it is steep and the hill is hard to climb, as the summit is not reached without many a fall, but how pure is the air when this level is reached! How many clouds cling to the lower levels that do not obscure the vision here!"

" You have given me something to think about. But while you were speaking I was thinking that it was possible for some lives to be of such a character that it would be exceedingly difficult to classify them. They might belong to one level one day, and to another the next."

"I think I know what you mean. I am very much afraid that sometimes I am a mere drifter, and very often I am on the look-out for Number One. Sometimes I get as high as the fourth level only to tumble down to the foot of the hill again. But it is always a good thing to aim high, anyway."

# CHAPTER XVII.

## *THE PERSISTENT LOVER.*

"Oh, dear! There is that horrid calf in again! It has broken a board off the fence, too. I don't think Mr. Green ought to be allowed to have that thing on the road; it's always getting into somebody's place. May, come and help get this calf out of the garden."

After calling her little sister, who, eager for the chase, at once ran out of the house, Helen began to drive the four-footed robber out of the lot. "May, open the gate and don't let the brute go past it, whatever you do."

The calf looked at first with cool disdain at his opponent, then helped himself liberally to the green corn, which he appeared to think was planted solely for his benefit. A small stone thrown at him only caused him to wag his tail, as if he were brushing away a saucy mosquito; after doing this he tramped on still farther into the patch, pulling stalks out by the roots and hastily devouring them on his way. A blow with an immense stick, wielded with considerable vigor, made him realize that he was wanted to go somewhere or to do something. But he only went farther among the sweet stalks, seeming to take a fiendish pleasure in destroying as much as he could. At last, after fully one-half of the corn had been destroyed, Helen was able to get the calf away from his delicious treat, but he seemed unable to see the gate, although a much smaller opening would have been plainly visible had he been on the outside of the fence, instead of the inside. At last, after he had investigated a cabbage patch, taken a few bites to see if the cabbages were a good kind, and had pruned a few apple trees, although not according to any scientific method, he finally condescended to make his exit, to the very great relief of Helen and May.

The former then proceeded to repair the fence where it had been broken. While thus engaged, she was startled by hearing a voice, in which there was a slight suspicion of laughter, say:

"Which are you trying to hit, the nail or your thumb? Let me help you, won't you?"

The speaker was a tall, broad-shouldered young man of twenty-five, whose broad forehead and clear grey eyes denoted intelligence, and tightly pressed lips and squarely-built jaw, determination.

Dick Hardy had now been with his uncle, Philip Hastings, four months, long enough to be on very friendly terms with his young neighbor, who at seventeen, was a much better-looking young lady than her childish looks had foretold.

An angry flush appeared on Helen's face, as she went on hammering without even looking up from her occupation. But Dick was never easily daunted, so he went on:

"I say, Helen, that is the third time you hit that poor thumb of yours, and the nails you have managed to drive in are not straight. You're a first-class cook, that I can vouch for, but you'll never make a

carpenter.  Come, don't be a goose; let me fix the
fence."

"I was getting on all right until you came along
and bothered me.  Please go away, and leave me
alone."

The only answer to this rude speech was a firm
but gentle grasp of the two hands of the would-be
carpenter and the speedy possession of her tools.
Helen stood in dignified silence, as Dick took out
nearly all the nails she had driven with so much
trouble and suffering, then firmly hammered the
board to the posts.

" There!  That won't come off very easily now,
I guess," said he, as he stood back surveying his
work with satisfaction.

" Thank you," said Helen, rather ungraciously, as
she reached out her hand for the hammer and nails.

" No, I'll take care of these.  I'm not going away
yet.  I came to have a serious talk with you and I
mean to have it.  What have I done or said that you
should be treating me so coolly?  We have been
such good friends until the last two weeks.  What's
wrong, anyway?"  And the honest grey eyes looked
keenly into the drooping face of the girl.

" Nothing," was the answer, as she turned her face
away.

" Now, don't tell fibs.  If you won't tell me, I
shall tell you.  You know that I love you and you
have tried to keep me from telling you so.  Why, I
don't know, but I am going to find out.  I've told
you now, in spite of your late coolness.  Listen to
me.  I love you, Helen; will you be my wife?"  The
slight tremor in the voice, as the last words were

spoken, showed the earnestness of the speaker, who from his height of six feet looked down with flushed face upon the trembling form of the girl, who was trying to shield her face from the keen gaze of the persistent lover.

"No, no, please don't ask me! I don't mean to get married at all."

"Why not, pray?"

"Can you ask me such a question? Do you suppose that I shall carry my shame into another family?"

"Shame? I do not understand you."

"You are not generally so dense. Why do you torture me so? I am not going to have any man, for my sake, feel that he lowered himself by marrying the daughter of a man who left his wife to marry another woman." Saying this, Helen burst into tears, bitter, scalding tears, which were now accompanied by sobs that shook her slender frame.

Pain at her suffering and pleasure that it was not from any feeling of aversion towards himself that induced Helen to refuse his offer, struggled for mastery in the bosom of the young man as he stood, allowing nature to take her course for a while before he answered:

"Nonsense! Helen, I thought you were a sensible girl. You are not responsible for your father's faults. He is not a criminal, and even if he were, I should, and so would any right-minded man, feel honored by having for a wife such a noble girl as yourself. My uncle is aware of my feelings towards you and wishes me success in my wooing, saying that he regards me as a son and that he will be delighted to welcome you for a daughter.  I have told you that I love you; now I wish to know your feelings towards me.  Do you love me, Helen?"

"What can a girl of seventeen know about love?"

"I am not going to be put off by such an evasive speech.  Look me in the face and give me a plain answer to a plain question.  Do you love me—yes or no?"

Two minutes that seemed like two hours to the anxious lover passed before the girl slowly raised her blushing face and said, "I can't say 'no' and I am not sure that I should say 'yes.'  It would do no good, for I have fully made up my mind to be an 'old maid.'"

"Thank God for the crumb of comfort you have given me.  Do you suppose that I shall be satisfied until I obtain the whole loaf?  Time will tell which is the stronger, my love or your foolish pride.  Good-bye."

It was not until Dick had left her that Helen fully understood her own feelings.  She had been quite honest when she told Dick that she was not sure she should say "yes," but now that he had gone half vexed, but still determined to win her, she realized that he had a larger place in her heart than even her mother, dearly as she loved her.  But this realization, although it added to her suffering, did not make her swerve from her resolution to live a life of single blessedness.

# CHAPTER XVIII.

## *LIGHT AT EVENTIDE.*

AND how was Guy Pierce getting on all this time? Not very well. As soon as his father, an honorable English gentleman, heard that he had, after getting a divorce on insufficient grounds, married again, he immediately wrote to Guy a very angry letter, saying that his son was to look for no further help from him, as the former was a disgrace to his family. At the time Pierce received this letter the scales had fallen from his eyes. Indeed, he had not been married a month before he began to compare his new wife with his former one, much to the discredit of the new one. During one of the numerous quarrels between the couple, Mrs. Pierce, in her desire to annoy her husband said:

"I suppose you wonder why you never heard from your Mary during your illness. Would you like to know why?"

"I suppose Philip Hastings knows more about that than either you or I. Curse him for a sneaking interloper!"

"Save your curses for someone else, my dear Guy. It amuses me to think how easily you were fooled."

"Fooled? What do you mean, woman?"

"Woman! A while ago it was 'dear Julia.' If I were not getting tired of you I would not tell you something that will make you wish yourself back with your saintly wife in Ortgeard.  Do you want to hear it?"

"Out with it then!  I don't know that anything can make me feel more wretched than I do now."

"Well, you did not hear from your wife for the good reason that your letters never left my house. Not knowing your new address, she could not very well write to you?"

"Do you mean that you did not post my letters to her?"

"Yes, I posted them—in the grate," she said with a heartless laugh.

"How could you do such a cruel thing as that? But that letter from your friend—did you write that yourself?"

"No, I am not quite so clever as that, and I have not yet added forgery to my list of crimes.  That was a *bona fide* letter, but my friend was mistaken in thinking that the first Mrs. Pierce was such a wicked woman as to think more of any one else than of her own husband.  No, she leaves such wickedness to her once most worthy husband, and is now regarded in Ortgeard as a saintly martyr, and her husband—that was—as the vilest of men."

"Good heavens!  What a fool I have been ever to believe a word against poor Mary!  If you are telling me the truth—" he paused.

"Well, what then?  She is welcome to you, as I intend suing for a divorce from a man that can't keep himself, and has lost most of his good looks!"

"The sooner you do so the better I shall be satisfied.  Would to God I had never seen your false face that lured me to destruction!"

"Do you think for one moment that your darling will have anything to do with you now? In the last letter I got from Ortgeard I was told that she was not expected to live, so if you want to sue for her love and forgiveness you'd better hurry."

Mrs. Julia Pierce never forgot the look that her victim gave her as he left the room and house never to return. But his departure appeared to be a source of congratulation to her, as it aided her in getting the divorce she was now so anxious to obtain, so she could marry a richer man who had lately taken her fancy.

Summer had passed, and October with its wealth of rosy-cheeked apples, had come, still Mrs. Mary Pierce lingered on. Some days her friends had hopes of her recovery, but she herself never wavered in her belief that death would soon claim her for his prey. Although late in the month, the air was so pleasant and balmy that the patient was sitting in a comfortable Morris-chair on the verandah when Philip Hastings came with the mail, which he quietly handed to the invalid, then sat down on the steps for a chat. A hasty exclamation from his companion caused him to look up. The injured wife was reading a letter that seemed to affect her deeply.

"Poor Guy!" at last she said. "I knew that somebody must have grossly slandered me to him before he would have cast me off. Thank God that his eyes have been opened before it was too late!"

"Too late for what?"

"For our reconciliation. Here is his letter. Read it and you will pity him as I do."

"Pity him I may, but forgive—never!" So saying he took the letter and calmly read its contents, after which he sat awhile in deep thought before he spoke.

"What is your wish in the matter, Mary?"

"To telegraph at once to him, telling him to come home, that all is forgiven. Oh, please send the telegram at once, tell him to come as soon as he possibly can, for the time is short! I must see him before I die!"

"Very well, I shall do so at once," and Philip Hastings returned to the town and sent the telegram. He even exceeded his friend's instructions, for, suspecting the impecunious condition of the prodigal, he told him to telegraph for money if any was needed. Before he left the office he received a telegram from Pierce with the words, "Coming at once!" With this telegram he hastened to Ferncliff, for he knew the state of anxiety in which he had left the patient was very unfavorable to her recovery.

The news that her husband was returning seemed to give new life to Mary Pierce, and the doctor said that there was now a chance of her restoration to health. In less than a week she might expect him who had so cruelly wronged her, but whom she loved with all the intensity of a strong nature. But if it had not been for the fear of wounding her mother's feelings, Helen would have expressed her indignation at her father's daring to return to the home whose happiness he had wrecked. She had not told her mother of her refusal of Dick Hardy's offer of marriage, but the young fellow himself had disclosed the secret. Mrs. Pierce, loving Dick already as a son,

often pondered on the best means of leading Helen
to reconsider her decision.  After the receipt of the
letter that partially excused her father's conduct,
Helen had a long talk with her mother, which tended
to soften somewhat her feelings towards her father,
although she still seemed unwilling to give any sat-
isfactory promise to Dick.  How true it is that we do
not rise or fall alone, but that our lives are so closely
interwoven with those of others that we cannot commit a wrong without causing sorrow and suffering to
many innocent lives!

Great was the astonishment that prevailed in
Ortgeard when the citizens learned of the second
divorce and expected arrival of Mr. Pierce.  Had it
not been for the tact of Mr. Hastings, whom all respected, and for the love and sympathy that all felt
for Mrs. Pierce, the reception given to the offender
on his arrival at Ortgeard Wharf would have been a
very stormy one.

Philip Hastings kindly offered to meet Pierce at
the wharf, so that the latter might not feel that he
was altogether an outcast in Ortgeard.

" Welcome back to Ortgeard," were the kind words
that greeted the wreck of the once handsome Guy
Pierce as he landed on Ortgeard Wharf.  Although
five years younger than Philip, Guy looked now at
least ten years older, so much had sickness and remorse aged him.  They had also humbled him, or he
would not have returned to meet the scornful looks of
those who he feared would either quietly ignore
him or publicly insult him.  He was greatly relieved
when he saw his acquaintance of former years with a

handsome carriage ready to convey him speedily to his wife and children.

"How is she?" were his first words, as he clasped the hands of his former rival, who was now showing himself to be his best friend.

"She seems a little better since she received your letter, but the doctor fears that it is only a temporary improvement. Be prepared to see a great change in her."

"Is—is there no hope of her recovery?" the anxious husband stammered.

"Very little, I fear. If anything will cure her your return will do it!"

"I owe you an apology for believing you guilty of trying to corrupt the honor of my wife. I should have known you better than to doubt your integrity. But jealousy and my infatuation for that woman—I cannot call it love—appear to have blinded me."

"I must be honest with you, Mr. Pierce. After your divorce I did tell your wife of my love for her and begged her to marry me. But previous to that not a word passed my lips that I should have been ashamed or afraid for you or any one else to hear; not a glance from my eyes that I should have been afraid for any one to see. I shall tell you what she said when I made her that offer, so you may know how noble is the woman you deserted. She said that she loved you still and that she had regarded me only as a friend. Think of this, Guy Pierce, and ask yourself if you were ever worthy such true, unalterable love?"

The last sentence was said very sternly, for poor Philip could not help feeling that Guy was being

treated better than he deserved, although for Mary's
sake he had resolved to be a true friend to him now
when he would be in need of friends.

"No, I was never worthy of her, but I always
loved her even when I thought I loved another. I
love her more than ever now, and mean to show that
love by devoting the rest of my life to her comfort
and happiness."

The arrival of the two men at Ferncliff prevented
any further conversation between them.

Sad, but yet joyful, was the meeting between husband and wife, for what they were in fact a short
ceremony made them by law.

Mr. Pierce was a changed man; he appeared to
think no trouble too great to take for the sake of her
who had suffered so much through him. Even Helen,
who was inclined to be cold and critical, could not
resist his kindness and appealing looks, and returned
the affection that was now lavishly bestowed upon her
as well as upon her brother and sister. The week
following the return of the husband and father was
a very happy one to the Pierce family. Even the
doctor began to look more cheerful when he visited
his patient.

Miss Todd was delighted when she came to see the
change for the better in her friend, but her keen eyes
soon discovered something wrong with Helen, and
she soon found out from Mrs. Pierce what it was.
Her active mind then conceived a scheme for aiding
the happiness of the two young people who were her
especial favorites. She knew Helen too well to believe that she would acknowledge her love for Dick
while he remained coolly aloof. She accordingly pre-

pared to aid Cupid by inviting the lovers to tea one evening. Neither of them knew that the other was invited, and so skilfully did she plan that she was able to have an important conversation with Helen, while Dick was placed where he could, himself unseen, hear what was said. Not until he heard Helen's voice did he suspect the stratagem.

"Why do you bother me, dear Miss Todd? I tell you I mean to be a home girl; my mother will always be delicate and will need me. You are the nicest woman I know, except my mother, that is, and I think it would be fine to be a nice old maid like you!"

"Thank you for the compliment. But you have no right to sacrifice the life-long happiness of another for the sake of a whim. It would please your mother much more to see you happy than to see you trying to destroy that love which God has planted in your heart, that love which you have acknowledged to your mother, although you refuse to acknowledge it to him who is thirsting for it!"

"Oh, I don't think his thirst is very great. He appears to be very well satisfied with matters as they are. I don't believe he loves me a bit now."

"You don't, eh? You little minx! You told your mother you loved me, and you've got to tell me," were the words that greeted the ears of the proud girl as she was folded in the arms of him who she thought was at his own home.

Miss Todd, feeling that her presence was not desirable, quietly left the room, feeling well satisfied with the success of her stratagem.

The hopes of Mrs. Pierce's friends seemed in a
fair way of realization, when one evening after retir-
ing to her room she startled her husband by making
a strange gurgling noise.    He turned in terror to
catch his wife as she was falling to the floor.    A
stream of blood was issuing from her mouth, and her
face was almost as white as the pillows of the bed
upon which he gently placed her.    Fortunately there
was a telephone in the house, so no time was lost in
summoning the doctor to her aid, although to the
agonized family the few minutes previous to his
arrival seemed hours.    When he arrived he comforted the anxious ones somewhat by saying that the
hemorrhage was only slight and was not in itself
necessarily fatal.    "But," he added, " in her weak
condition it is, I fear, the precursor of death.    The
action of the heart is, indeed, very feeble!"

By the use of oxygen the doctor was enabled to re-
store his patient to consciousness, and before he left
she was able to speak.

As he was leaving the doctor was stopped by
Pierce who, with trembling lips, asked:

"Is there hope, doctor?   Can you not save her for
us by remaining with her for the rest of the day?"

The doctor shook his head.    "I have done my best.
I am not God and cannot prevent death from claim-
ing its victim when it is the Master's will to take
her to Himself.   I have shown you how to administer
the oxygen in case of need, and I shall return this
afternoon.   I cannot stay longer now, for I have other
patients to whom I can be of more use than to your
wife, who, unless I am mistaken, will not live to see
another sunrise."

" What has caused this illness ?"

" You ask me that!" said the doctor, with flashing eyes. "I tell you, man, you might better have stabbed that loving wife of yours to the heart with a sword than have done such a dastardly trick as you did. You knew the delicate constitution of your wife and her loving, sensitive nature, and yet you left her to suffer enough to kill a much stronger woman than she is. Science has made wonderful progress, but it has not yet discovered a remedy for a broken heart." So saying, he left the house, leaving his patient's husband the prey to the severest mental agony he had ever endured.

How is it that even those who doubt the personality of God, in times of deep distress, cry to Him for help! When the depths of a man's heart are stirred the Creator of the Universe is no longer to him a mere force, but a Person who can feel for His wayward children.

" O God!" the wretched man moaned, as he sat with head bowed upon his arms upon the table, trying, Jacob-like, to drive a bargain with his Maker; " save Mary's life and I'll serve You the rest of my life !"

A slight stir in the adjoining room caused him to return to the bedside of his wife. She looked up with a slight smile.

" Please don't leave me now, dear Guy. You won't need to stay—much longer!"

" Oh, Mary! Mary, don't die and leave me to be a murderer! I cannot, cannot let you go !"

" God's will—must be done. He has been—very kind to—give you back to me—before calling me to

Himself.  You have made me—very happy this week, darling.  God will—"

Her voice failed and her breath came in short, fitful gasps.  Hurriedly her husband administered oxygen, and was soon rewarded by seeing her revive. He feared to talk any more to her, and she soon fell asleep.  Her breath now came quite easily, and Guy began to feel that God was going to answer his petition, the first prayer, if prayer it could be called, he had offered since childhood.

The doctor came according to promise early in the afternoon, but his verdict was not encouraging.  Not since morning had the patient spoken.  She appeared to be fast sinking into a comatose condition.  Mr. Hastings and Dick Hardy came over at three o'clock, but seeing they could be of no use were about to leave the sick-room when Mrs. Pierce slowly opened her eyes and motioned for them to remain.  She tried to speak, and the restorative, which was at once given, soon enabled her to do so.

"You—won't mind—staying with me, will you, just—a little while?  Where's Helen?"

"Here, mother," was the answer, as Helen came where her mother could see her.

"Come—close, and Dick, too!  It's—all right— between you—now, isn't it?  Give me—your hands." Feebly she clasped their warm hands together in hers, now becoming cold, and said, "Be good—to— each other.  Kiss me—both."

Their eyes filled with tears as they at once complied with her request, then withdrew from the bedside to make room for Mr. Hastings, to whom she now bade farewell.

"May God bless you—for all your kindness—to me and mine. Helen will be—a daughter to you. Good—night—'twill be good morning when—we meet again!"

A few minutes passed when nothing could be heard but the sobs of the sorrowing friends. At last, with a supreme effort, the dying woman turned to her husband, who was kneeling beside the bed, and said:

"Don't fret, I'm happy—so happy. Heaven's gate—is ajar for you. We shall—meet again. I know, for God—has told me so. You—won't be—lonely, for I—"

But exhausted nature could do no more, and the sentence remained unfinished.

When the last rays of the setting sun shone into the room they rested upon the marble, but smiling, face of Mary Pierce, to whom the injustice of British Columbia law had caused such bitter suffering.